Potomac Review

Potomac Review is a journal of fiction, poetry, and nonfiction
published by the Paul Peck Humanities Institute at
Montgomery College, Rockville
51 Mannakee Street, Rockville, MD 20850

Potomac Review has been made possible through
the generosity of Montgomery College.

A special thanks to Dean Rodney Redmond.

For submission guidelines and more information:
www.potomacreview.org

Potomac Review, Inc. is a not-for-profit 501 c(3) corp.
Member, Council of Literary Magazines & Presses
Indexed by the American Humanities Index
ISBN: 978-0-9990403-3-1
ISSN: 1073-1989

SUBSCRIBE TO POTOMAC REVIEW
One year at $24 (2 issues)
Two years at $36 (4 issues)
Sample copy order, $12 (single issue)

TABLE OF CONTENTS

FICTION

POETRY

Nonfiction

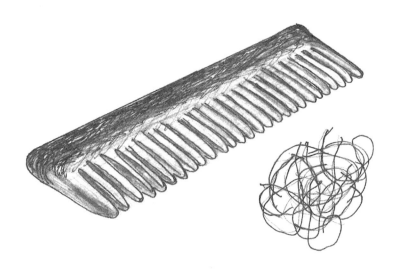

What could be a better reflection of a woman than the
parts of her body she so carelessly throws away?

KARLEE NEBRASKA

Hush sweet baby;
Don't cry your eyes.
Soon you'll return,
to that sweet paradise.

Washed in the blood,
washed in the blood,
washed in the blood of the lamb.

Natalie

As her soft membranes began to break, Natalie did her best to walk, balancing the whole of her body first on the round bottoms of her heels, then slowly to the swollen pads below her toes, one foot first, one foot first.

The pain was not where she expected. She had had a child before, and this was different. With Ruthie, the pain was in her back, a hollow wave that rippled down to her butt. She had not expected that pain either because she had watched so many shows and movies about pregnant women with Anthony, a happy ritual that had developed around the promise of parenthood. In these movies, women glowed and hummed happy lullabies, and pregnancy was difficult for them in a slapstick sort of way. The birthing process usually involved women always looking down at their stomachs or vaginas, as if the pain they were feeling was something like going to the bathroom, a matter of just getting the big thing out of you, and not something else, not a wave of pain in your back and all throughout that just clutches all your cells.

The pain was in her back with Ruthie, not her stomach, a stomach that sagged low, framed by a rippling layer of fat and scar tissue. Now the pain was in her legs—from her butt to her knees—and the doctor wanted her to walk on these legs that burned as if her bones were burning from the marrow out. She pushed around the room, teetering on those two hollow ovens while her bones turned to ash and ember. The doctor said she must break her water, but she felt dried up. There was no water. The baby had taken all of it. Burned it up.

Kathy

Kathy sat in the waiting room of the hospital, scrolling down her phone passively with her left thumb. The nail on her thumb was broken, the light blue polish chipping around the frame of her nail bed. It had been more than three weeks since her last manicure. She would have to remember to make an appointment soon. She was just beginning to remember how to be herself again: how much a chipped manicure used to mean to her, how important it used to be to check the mail, how often she used to water her plants. She was just beginning to decide that it was all so silly, behaving like a ghost for so long after breaking up with Steven.

During dinner with her sister, she talked about this, and Natalie had been unusually receptive, nodding her head with a friendly energy. It was almost like Kathy was talking to a friend.

"You know, I've always admired you," Natalie told her.

Natalie rarely talked to Kathy about her feelings. Even their dinner together seemed strange to Kathy, Natalie's idea. Completely out of the blue.

"Here I am, telling you that I have to remind myself how to water my plants, and you come back with 'I admire you.' Are you okay?"

"Oh, you know. Hormones."

Sometime after dessert and coffee, Natalie realized she was having contractions. They walked around the block for thirty anxious minutes before Kathy convinced Natalie to let her drive her to the hospital.

Ruthie

With the soft palm of her hand, Ruthie pushed down the little gray stick of a lock that protruded from the summit of her door. She felt as if she had pushed her hand into a peanut butter sandwich. She stared at the filthy palm of her hand as if the staring would make her clean again. Then, because she knew she could do nothing else, she pulled the lock up with her nimble fingers; she pulled hard until the terrible little lock clicked into place, and then she deliberately pushed it back down with the palm of her hand. This time, the noise of the motions made her feel guilty; her stomach flopped like a freshly caught catfish.

And now she was hesitant to pull the lock up again and push it back down because she was afraid. She stared at the lock, her hands gripping firmly, desperately, into the slippery seats of her father's car. She counted to seven.

Her chest began to split open. She could not stop herself. Too much had happened already. As she pulled up the lock, she no longer felt like she was breaking in half, and she was glad she had let herself indulge. Except, as she pushed the lock back down with the soft palm of her hand, she could feel her chest snap like a wishbone anyway, with that thin sort of asymmetrical pop. She knew that she had to do it again, and she knew that she would have to do it again after that, and she was already tired of herself, already tired of the possibility of the next four seconds of her life. The next four seconds, the idea of it was so exhausting.

Ruthie's father drove through the dark streets as a yellow bruise began to form on the bottom of her hand. She tried to concentrate on other sensations, on the cold hard seats of her father's car, so cold that her back and butt felt wet. She tried to think about where they were going (to the hospital, to the hospital, to the hospital) but the sour pain of her palm was persistent, and it was all she could think about. The murky lips of the night ate the light around the car, and Ruthie had trouble seeing anything but the lock and the beige iridescent cone of light from the headlights. The light itself pushed through the dark heavy air of the streets the way Ruthie had seen trucks push snow with their shovel heads.

She forced her mind to wander. Ruthie thought about light. She thought of the dark slush on the edges of the streets, and she thought of the beautiful noise slush makes underneath heavy plastic soles. She thought about how matter and light are made of the same things, and she wondered if light could gel or if it could melt, if she could ever hold light in her hands and push it against her face. She wondered if she could wash herself in light.

She thought about time, and she wondered if time was made of the same stuff as light and matter. She read somewhere that time did not exist inside a wormhole, and this thought made her think about what she would find if her small body were to crawl inside one. She imagined being frozen in space, and this was a beautiful thought. She would be something of a statue, a petrified fossil suspended in space — this stationary state implied a certain repetition she so often yearned for: life, life, life.

Then she imagined her body merely recreating the last four seconds of her life while she floated inside this wormhole, over and over, her motions trapped in time. This wormhole would take from her everything except the length and movement of her body. It would take from her the sound of her voice just before she could scream, just before the fifth second.

She was just pulling up the lock, her face full, pale, and wide, when her father opened her car door. His skyscraper body stood still long enough to allow Ruthie to pull up the lock before he opened the door, unbuckled her seatbelt, and pulled her into the cold, wet night. Ruthie could see that she and her father were at the hospital, the one she had gone to when she had swallowed those marbles, each one cold on her teeth, cold in her throat, cold in her deep stomach. But they were here to see Mother, Mother whose stomach was swollen and warm and full.

Kathy

Steven was texting her. Did he know she was at the hospital? Her mother probably posted something about it on Facebook. Kathy put away her phone.

She wanted Steven to forget she existed. It was the only way she could go back to normal. Except that Steven had been normal enough, and leaving him had made everything strange. After she broke up with him, she found herself walking around her life like a stranger, as if she were a substitute in a classroom. Simple remedial tasks — work emails, grocery shopping, doctor's appointments — seemed not only confusing, but also pointless. She thought that breaking up with Steven might make everything better. It only made things strange.

She told him over the phone. They had lived together, eating their breakfasts together, brushing their teeth together, yet she told him over the phone on her lunch break because she was a coward. Then she stayed at a hotel for two days so that he could pack his things. It was his idea for her to keep the apartment.

It was only more recently that she began to walk out of her fog, which allowed her to remember again all his problems: his smelly feet, his obsession with football, his wet teabags on her countertops. These were flaws that Natalie had told her to just accept.

"Your problem is that you expect to find a man that is made for you, like some kind of expensive dress," Natalie told her once over the phone.

"Well, I don't think there is anything wrong with having high standards," Kathy retorted, thumbing a tear in the wallpaper in her kitchen.

"Ha! High standards! Listen. He has a job. He has an education. He is fairly good looking. What else do you need?"

"I don't know. Maybe I need someone who has something to say to me."

"I don't even know what that means. What do you want him to say to you?"

"Don't be a bitch. You know what I mean." Kathy began to feel sick, her stomach suddenly gelatinous and unstable, her forehead and cheeks suddenly warm. She poured herself a glass of water and listened to her sister suck on her bottom lip for a few seconds.

"Things will be different when you have children together."

That conversation had been eight years ago, a year after she and Steven had moved in together. Nine years they had been together. Nine years with a man who never flossed his teeth. Nine years with a man who could not make grilled cheese. Nine years with a man who never came during her blow jobs. Now she was thirty-four. Now Natalie admired her.

She remembered feeling, just after she turned twenty-six, a persistent anxiety that chewed her brain like a gnawing gray beetle, and this gnawing had lasted until she turned twenty-eight, the year she finished her master's. How stupid she had been. Now she was thirty-four. Now Natalie admired her.

Kathy picked up one of the magazines on the end table beside her. She decided on a magazine marketed toward married women her age. Recipes, pictures of beautifully decorated homes, drinks that promised to melt away saddlebags. She skimmed the magazine, thinking absently about Natalie, about her large round belly and new baby.

She thought of a game she and Natalie always played as children. They liked to reenact scenes from movies, especially Disney movies. There was this scene in *Beauty and the Beast* where Belle would sing by a water fountain in the middle of her happy village. She held a book and sang to her sheep friends about the story she was reading, and while she sang, one of the sheep would nibble indifferently on the corner of one of the pages of her book. As a child, this was Natalie's favorite scene in the movie, and when they played together, Kathy would be made to play the part of the sheep. Kathy was never the princess, always instead some minor character, sometimes female.

"Bite the page."

"That isn't what Belle says. She says, 'Here is where she meets

Prince Charming.'"

"I already said that. Now you have to bite the page."

"I don't want to."

"You have to."

Kathy wondered if Natalie's new daughter would be the cunt Natalie had been, or maybe it was Ruthie who would turn out to be the cunt.

Natalie

The doctor told Natalie to walk around. It would make the water break. It would help with the pain. She didn't want to walk. She wanted to sit on the heels of her feet and hug her knees in toward her chest. This was the way she had learned to deal with menstrual cramps; a few tugs, a few breaths, and then it would pass, like all unpleasant things. She wanted to hold her legs to her chest, but her doctor told her to walk.

She thought about the way some celebrities gave birth, knees to chest, body shaped like an owl, inside a swimming pool, the kind Ruthie would play in in the summer in their front yard. It wasn't just celebrities. A girl from church, she had used a pool too, but Natalie still connected it to celebrities because she and Anthony had first heard about it while watching Conan together on the couch, before Ruthie, when her marriage was a collection of days on the couch before he would come home and a collection of evenings with him on the couch when he would return to her. Sometimes she cleaned; sometimes she read a book; sometimes she would buy something on Amazon. It had been that way for some time until Ruthie. She didn't work because she didn't have to, and she was fine with that. She didn't work, because she would be a mother, and she was fine with that too. That was so long ago.

Now it was cleaning, cleaning, cleaning. Cleaning because Ruthie was a nervous child and particular. If something was dirty, if something was strange. It was cooking too, but not the fancy meals she sometimes prepared before Ruthie, meals with rich

7

sauces and white wines. Now, it was always something simple, something with chicken because Ruthie was particular and lactose intolerant. Something simple because Ruthie had allergies.

And Anthony never returned to her after work anymore, always returning to Ruthie, his anxious squealing Siren. Ruthie was small and precious and nervous and sickly and sad; he could not help but love her with an intense intimacy that seemed to burn away all other intimacies that might have clung to him before Ruthie, like a flame to a spider's web. She could see Ruthie changing him, the way daughters must change their fathers, and Natalie would have forgiven him if only he had also seen that she was changing too.

He still made love to her the same way, after all these years, on his side, her cool back on his warm chest, with soft pulsations from behind that used to fold into her chest and arms but now made her nauseous. He teased her in the same loving way he had always teased her, pulling her in for a kiss only to tickle her under her arms, a game that had gotten so tired that now she pushed her elbows into her ribs any time he touched her.

One day, she had asked him to pick up some groceries after work, and he came home beaming, clearly proud of himself, with several bags of food. After leaving the bags on the counter, he left the kitchen to check on Ruthie.

When she put the groceries away, she found the cookies. They were in the very first bag she picked up, a green box of dark chocolate thin mints, a brand of cookie she used to hoard away in her early twenties. She had not eaten them in years, perhaps because after eating an entire sleeve during her pregnancy, she had thrown them up. And here they were on her counter, his gift to her. *You see*, he seemed to tell her, *I was thinking of you*.

That night she waited for him to go to sleep so that she could tool around the quiet of her house as she had done for so many nights. Without really thinking about her disgust or her exhaustion, in the neutral movement of a ghost, she took the cookies from the countertop and poured them into the garbage disposal. *They are not a present for me,* she thought. *They are a present for someone else.*

Ruthie

The nurse told them to make a left and to go straight through the gray heavy doors and walk until they saw the orange Y on the wall, and then make a right and walk a little more past about three or four rooms. Her mother's room would be there, just past those three or four rooms.

Ruthie looked down, though she tried to never look down, and she saw that the floor was made of white tiles, each square large enough to frame both of her feet. She walked very carefully, as if she were walking down a wedding aisle, left together, right together, left together, right together, making sure her feet stayed inside the thin black lines around the tile.

Her father waited at the end of the hall.

Kathy

Kathy read a story in her magazine.

It began with the hair from a woman's brush, the reporter wrote. After the woman's 60th birthday, she cleaned her hairbrush, pulling with her skinny, wizened fingers a thick mat of hair from the bristles. The day was hot and stagnant, he continued, the air that golden color that seems to reveal every microbe in the atmosphere. The woman must have examined the wad blankly, not really seeing it, having every intention of throwing it away.

She then began cleaning her brush daily, rolling the silver strands into a small, greasy ball with her wrinkled but still agile fingers and pressing the ball into a larger wad on her bedside table. Maybe she would throw it away soon, she would think. Maybe this is just silliness, a phase.

Now she pulls hair from the filter of her vacuum twice a week and adds her discovered treasures to one of the many balls of hair on her bedside table. The reporter had counted four balls, each the circumference of the palm of her hand, and she told the reporter that after she collected six, she would put them in a garbage bag in her closet. She also had a small mason jar in her medicine cabinet in which she stored her fingernails and toenails, which she trimmed once a week. In that same medicine cabinet, there was a long glass cylinder with two amber-colored stones floating in murky orange liquid.

"Kidney stones!" she revealed. "Apparently, people ask to keep them all the time."

The woman smiled with the certain chaotic wisdom just before blowing her nose and tossing the tissue into the wastebasket beside her bed, and the reporter wondered if the woman might soon start pulling these from wastebaskets and begin pressing them into scrapbooks the way teenagers might with their prom corsages.

Women collect things, the reporter continued: stamps on passports, letters, flowers, empty bottles, receipts, selfies, tattoos, scars, books, bruises. A woman is prone to believe that each item might be a reflection of her. Her pain. Her joy. Her youth. Her body. Yet what are we really but cells — skin and blood. What could be a better reflection of a woman than the parts of her body she so carelessly throws away?

Natalie

Natalie kept walking, lumbering her weight on her swollen feet, her swollen legs, her swollen body. She had once watched an Internet video of a woman who danced through her contractions, moving her hips lustfully to the beat of a very popular rap song. The woman had looked centered, confident.

Natalie had never learned to dance anything but the two-step, so each time the burning in her legs cooled to a manageable ache, she tried to sway about the room. Anthony had taught her to dance the two-step.

What had they been listening to that night? It was not the

song she was humming to herself just then. The song she hummed was a sad one that had just crept into her, something she heard somewhere, she could not remember, something she did not remember the lyrics to except for that last lonely line. *How my heart is now wondering no misery can tell. You left me no warning, no words of farewell.* When Anthony taught her the two-step, they had been listening to something different, something faster and sillier, and they had been laughing because of the irony. They were laughing because she was not a girl who danced the two-step, and he was a not a man who taught women how to dance. And the song was sublimely silly, something with words like *whiskey* and *wanna*. She could not remember the song, and she would not ask him about it, so she tried to push it out of her mind. She continued to sway self-consciously.

Ruthie

Ruthie tried to make her mind wander. She thought about marching wives and marching soldiers. She tried not to think about her feet, but she was already marching and she could only wait until it was over. She marched until she reached her mother's room, and then she marched past her mother's room until she reached the end of the hall, and because she could not stop herself, she turned left and marched until her father's skyscraper body picked her up off of the floor. He was always able to do this for her, to pull her away from the overwhelming truth of herself. She sank her head into his shoulder and started crying.

"What's wrong, Ruthie?"

She shook her damp face into his shirt.

"Are you tired?"

She pulled her face from his shoulder and nodded. He kissed her forehead.

He carried her to the door of her mother's room. They watched as her mother lumbered around the hospital room in her gown, her two red feet as large as frying pans, her fat hands gripping the back of her gown so that her behind would not peek out. She was humming something sad, something from the radio.

Her father laughed. Her mother screamed, and water fell onto the floor. Ruthie screamed too, and her eyes spilled water onto her cheeks.

Kathy

Anthony found her sleeping with the magazine folded around her pointer finger.

"They won't let Ruthie stay. Will you watch her?"

"Fine," mumbled Kathy before jolting forward violently, her eyes two white moons. She had been dreaming that she was in a hospital, and she had expected to wake up in her bed, a big warm bed with no Steven. She was just beginning to remember how wonderful it was to have her own bed. But she was still in a hospital. And now she was briefly terrified by the possibilities of her life. She could not remember which parts of her life were dreams and which parts had happened. She could not remember if she ever had a bed without Steven. She could not remember why she was in a hospital.

Natalie

They pushed a needle into her back, and he watched as they did it. She did not want him to watch. It was none of his business. She wanted to ask him to leave.

Ruthie

Ruthie sat in a chair in the waiting room beside her dozing aunt. If she squinted her eyes just right, she could see little piece of dust that glowed in the air around her, soaking in the fluorescent light. This glowing dust was everywhere, no matter how clean you made something, there was always dust you could breathe. But her father told her that it was a game, that you could squint just so and watch them float, and urge them to float somewhere specific. It was like betting on horses, he said, except your betting against yourself. All that made it better, made it easier to breathe. Her father made everything dirty clean, or cleaner.

Ruthie thought about her father as she watched a piece of golden dust land on the lightbulb beside her. Ruthie was going to have a new sister, and she wondered if her father would love this new sister. Ruthie hoped not. She hated new things, and even if he still loved Ruthie the same amount, she knew he could not love her in quite the same way. Her chest felt tight from her fear of this new thing — new love, new sister — she could not control it. No matter how loud she screamed, it would not change — new sister, new love. Ruthie hated new things.

The weight on her chest consumed her all at once. She did not want to lose control of her breathing in front of her aunt. She needed her father. She could not lose control of her breathing. Heaving, she walked across the room and lay her body down under the television in the waiting room and prop up her feet against the wall. Her palm was still warm from the car lock, so she pressed it into the floor as well and thought about the cold, how cold air seems to pinch, how cold bodies never rot, how cold water burns the teeth.

She saw a movie once where a man filled a bathtub with ice and froze himself asleep and woke up twenty years in the future. Was it a sad movie? She wished she could go back in time and make it so her mother was not pregnant. Or perhaps she could live in a world where her mother remained pregnant forever, perhaps slowly became more pregnant every day, changing in imperceptible little ways, growing large but not inconvenient. Ruthie was old enough to know that these were selfish thoughts, the kind of thoughts she would have to keep from her father. That was new too.

13

Kathy

Kathy walked into the black fog of the parking lot, pushing her hand into her purse for a lighter. She had left her niece in the waiting room, lying on the floor just under the television, her feet propped against the wall.

"Excuse me, nurse?"

The nurse had been reluctant to watch Ruthie. She would only be a second, Kathy had promised, just a second. Just a second to gather herself in the space of the night, the space that had collected around her. The nurse told her that it was not her job to watch a stranger's child.

"I know you are very busy. I'll only be a second."

Kathy knew that if she left, the nurse would watch Ruthie. She knew that whatever she did, no matter how much the nurse protested, she would still be able to leave, and Ruthie would be watched over. The key was to do just what you wanted to do. The nurse would be unhappy regardless.

She smoked urgently, as if she needed to prove a point to someone about her need for this cigarette. She grew suddenly lightheaded and nauseous, her head and stomach full of smoke. She wanted to sit down, but that would have been embarrassing, even if there was no one around to see her sitting in the vast blackness of the parking lot. Even if no one saw her, she would still know that she had sat down on the cold pavement, lightheaded from one cigarette. She would feel old and silly, sitting on this frozen asphalt.

Kathy remembered her first cigarette after quitting for something like six months.

"It's good to quit smoking before you get pregnant," her sister had said to her smugly.

"Who say's I'm getting pregnant?"

Kathy began to feel nauseous again. When was her last period? She threw the rest of her cigarette into the parking lot and walked back inside the hospital.

Anthony
Karlee was born with straight, black hair and eyes like blue tile.

   Karlee was born with red skin that stretches thin across her small face.

   He could see through her translucent skin, could see the blood that pushed around her body, could see the pulse of her skin against her bones. He rocked Karlee Nebraska carefully, and he was happy because he was the first to hold his new baby daughter. They had tried to give her to Natalie, but Natalie was tired, so tired.

   He wanted Ruthie to see her small resplendent body and her blue eyes, and he wanted Ruthie to hold her into her chest, the way he was holding her. He kissed his new daughter's eyes and cried and whispered nonsense into her forehead until his heart believed it was hollow.

   His world was something new. His world was filled with Karlee.

Ruthie
Ruthie lay on the cold floor of the waiting room and watched the lines of the baseboards. If she stared long enough, she could see herself balance along those lines, and she could see the lines move into the universe forever, and she could see her dark body walking through space.

   The tops of her thumbs felt heavy, as if something had propped itself on the nail beds, so she rubbed the tops of her thumbs with her pointer fingers over and over and over until she no longer thought of the weight of her thumbs. Her aunt Kathy had just returned with a Styrofoam cup of coffee in her hand. Ruthie knew her aunt was eyeing her, wondering what the fuss about her thumbs could possibly be, and Ruthie felt suddenly like a goldfish.

   "What are you doing?" Kathy laughed, not cruelly, but it was enough for Ruthie to push her hands into her armpits.

"I'm not doing anything," she mumbled.

"Fine, have it your way," Kathy chirped. "But if you are trying to snap your fingers, you are doing it wrong." Kathy pulled up her left hand to her ear, her thumb and middle finger pressing together firmly, and then, all at once, she snapped her fingers, making a terribly pleasant POP!

Ruthie grinned. "Do it again."

"Not until you get off the floor. For someone so afraid of being dirty, I don't see how you can stand to lie down on that floor."

"The floor isn't dirty."

"How do you know?"

"Because it isn't."

"Just get over here."

Ruthie pulled her body off the floor and sat down in a gray cushioned chair beside her aunt. Aunt Kathy smelled faintly sour, like bread dough, and her hair was tied up in a greasy, tangled bun. Kathy's hair was normally pulled back tight and clean, and her usual smell was the heavy musk of perfume aisles. Her skin was different too, the wrinkles around her mouth and the dark circles around her eyes were more pronounced. But Ruthie liked the way she looked and smelled, like something tired and wild.

"Now show me," Ruthie demanded.

"Well aren't we a little Miss Bossy Pants," Kathy sang, her voice long and playful.

"Please!" Ruthie pleaded.

POP! Kathy snapped her fingers again, this time mere inches in front of Ruthie's bright eyes.

"How did you do that?"

"It's easy. How old are you anyway?"

"I'll be eight in four weeks."

"Eight! Well I'm pretty sure I learned how to snap my fingers before that! What do you learn at school anyway?"

"I don't go to school."

"Aw, yes. Right."

Kathy

Kathy cleared her throat and pulled her fingers to her mouth in thought. She was grateful that her sister was not around to hear that question, evidence of her disconnection from the affairs of her sibling's awkward life. Her distance from her sister was Kathy's deliberate decision, yet she did not like being reminded of the space between them. *It was hard with sisters*, Kathy would tell others, tell herself, *especially my sister*.

She remembered again that Ruthie was homeschooled, her brother-in-law's idea. He said she was gifted. *Hardly, gifted*, Kathy thought to herself, *she can't even snap her fingers*.

"Show me again," Ruthie bossed, her face urgent.

"Say please."

"Please."

Kathy snapped her fingers again.

"Now your turn."

"I can't."

"You didn't even try."

Ruthie rubbed the middle finger of her right hand with her thumb for a few seconds and then presented her hand in defeat.

"I can't do it!"

Kathy rolled her eyes.

"Just practice. You will figure it out."

Kathy thought about how Ruthie might have been different if she had been her child. To begin with, she would go to school. Kathy didn't think it was right for children to spend so much time with their parents. She wondered if things would change after this new one. Would Natalie insist on some kind of reprieve?

Then again, if Ruthie were hers, she would also be Steven's. What an exhausting thought.

Anthony

Anthony watched his wife sleep. They had taken Karlee from him, taken her to the nursery for some vague reason that annoyed him. Why couldn't they wait until Natalie woke up? She would want to hold her daughter.

He looked at his wife, caressing the smooth lines of her hands while she slept. She looked younger than most women her age. It was not just her face, but her body too. Her breasts were still round and upright, not long and low like his friends' wives. Her butt had not flattened out like a large pancake either. She was always complaining about her body because her stomach had grown soft, full of scars and dimples, but he did not mind. He had always been an ass man anyway. He knew that he was lucky because he still wanted her the way he wanted her when they were first married. And anyway, she had given him so much.

He could feel the air being punched out of him from his loving her so much. No man could be so lucky. *No man*, he thought, *could have my beautiful daughters and my beautiful wife and not also know the tragedy that life implies. Someday, I will have to pay for all of this.*

Ruthie

Ruthie practiced snapping her fingers for several minutes until her middle finger began to throb like a heartbeat. *This is the sort of thing sisters teach each other*, Ruthie thought. *I have to learn things and teach them to her.* Ruthie knew she wouldn't be good at it. She knew before she could think those thoughts herself, before she knew the words she needed to think the thoughts she already understood.

Ruthie spent much of her life being scared of a door knob or obsessing over the number of crayons in her pencil box. She couldn't tie her shoes because it took her hours to get it right, and she didn't know anything except what she had read in books. Her mother didn't like listening to her talk about how leaves changed color or about the atoms in a hair follicle. Her sister would probably hate her too.

Ruthie continued to snap her fingers, her fingers turning red, her yellow palm turning blue. Her aunt chirped on the phone beside her.

Kathy

"Another daughter!" Kathy sang over the phone.

"Poor Anthony. He will be surrounded by women!"

Kathy rolled her eyes. Why did everyone say this, as if a house full of women were a cruel and unusual punishment? Even Natalie had said it at dinner.

"I'm sure it was hard for you and Dad," Kathy chided.

"Oh honey, you know what I mean."

Kathy looked down at her hands and started chipping off the rest of her blue polish from her thumb. She would have to get a manicure soon.

Natalie

Natalie slept more deeply than she ever remembered sleeping. The sound of such sleep, if one had to pin it down, is the sound of a drop of water falling into a hollow drum, a deep wet echo. The taste of such a sleep is a sort of sour taste that clings to the middle of the tongue and the roof of the mouth. The smell of such a sleep is warm and dry, the sort of smell that uses all of the nose and saturates the throat. It was the kind of sleep where one forgets they are alive, and this forgetting leaves no remorse, no wish to remember what was forgotten.

The sheets of the hospital bed stuck to her wet skin, and part of the white cotton sheet had gotten tucked under her back so that when she wiggled about on the bed in her slumber, the sheet tightened around her, trapping one of her arms to her side. Even with her arm pinioned to her side, she did not wake up, but continued to sleep as she wiggled. Her body asked her, asked her quite urgently, to pull her arm out of the sheet, but because she was asleep, she could not move them, not by asking them at least. Soon she was wiggling much more, and she was beginning to wake up because the violence of her body, the moisture of her skin, and the immobility of her arm had become a horrific mixture of existence, and it is difficult to sleep, however deeply, when the horror of one's body is screaming into them. Soon she was awake enough to will her other arm to pull at the sheet, but because she did not know to first open her eyes, this arm only grabbed at the sheet blindly, tightening it further.

She pulled the sheet around her with such a force that her entire body rotated into the blanket, making it tighter still. Now she was somewhere between sleep and consciousness. Vaguely, between these layers, she thought of her father, who would tuck her in at night by pushing her blanket very tightly around her body on either side of her, first her shoulders, then her torso, then her legs and feet, until she was immobile. She thought of the warm darkness around her after he would turn off the light in her bedroom.

She had never liked playing this game, but she played it anyway because she loved her father so desperately. His warm arms, his warm eyes, his warm face. He even made the darkness warm.

Anthony
Karlee Nebraska has a small pink face and eyes like a swimming pool.
Karlee Nebraska has a body made of glass.

Ruthie
"Is she mine?" Ruthie asked. Ruthie held her sister carefully in her arms. The baby had been bathed and wrapped in a blanket. She was perfectly clean, and Ruthie had never seen anything so beautiful, not even in her books about the universe.

"Yes, Ruthie. She is yours, but you have to share her with me, okay?" her father said, kissing Ruthie's forehead. Ruthie nodded. Karlee would be hers and his; they would share her. Ruthie's body ached with the truth of it. Everything dirty her father made clean.

Kathy

Kathy stood in the doorway, watching her brother-in-law holding both of his daughters. Natalie, who looked so small and warped, like a bird with broken wings, lay on the bed, tangled in her thin hospital blankets.

Kathy walked over to the bed and shook her sister awake.

"Natalie, is there anything you need?"

"Mom?"

"No. Mom is still in California. Where she lives? Natalie?"

Natalie's body was a stiff warm corpse.

"I'm so tired," Natalie groaned. "When did you get here?

"I've been here the entire time. I drove you to the hospital."

"Right." Natalie closed her eyes again.

Kathy looked over at her brother-in-law. He smiled brightly over his daughters, while Ruthie touched the cheeks of her infant sister.

Anthony looked up at Kathy and smiled. He lifted his new child's tiny hand and moved it back and forth as if the child were waving. As if the child knew her already and was happy to see her.

"Say hello to Aunt Kathy. Don't worry. She isn't as scary as she looks."

"Ha ha," Kathy choked before breaking into sobs. And now she was crying for reasons she barely understood, and it did not feel good to cry.

CHARLENE LANGFUR

UNGRASPABLE AND MIRACULOUS

This is how I've sketched it for today
with my yellow #2 pencil, each flower petal
unique as none of them are exactly the same.
The petals feel good in between my fingers,
smooth, inviting, honest, it helps me keep track of what
is around me, a gay woman growing flowers and herbs
and desert plants growing exactly as they do here in the middle
of the desert, and me saving their seeds in small glass
kitchen jars, calculating possible life spans on a calculator,
thinking they will last longer than I can imagine they will.
Life is inside them. The same as in me. The flowers show this,
show it comes back and back like the trees covered
with green oranges readying to become fully ripe. Orange and
sweet. I think love is the same, the love shown me long ago is
still with me, shines in me even now, all the brilliant parts still stick,
how you stood up legs and arms akimbo in the morning light,
declaring what love for another woman was for you and how
days later, how it was gone, fallen through all the cultural and
sociological cracks, fallen so deep you could not get the love back,
but I held on, gardening and taking to new pencil sketches and
making new lists of what worked, of what connected us and what
didn't. Hoping to get it back. Even now I can describe how
your eyes glistened and the curls on your forehead fell over
your forehead. The cloudy sky fell away on the day it worked
for us for the first time. It was the real deal and we both knew it.
I stayed until there was no more to go on, until it made no sense
and then another year passed and another. The giant
sunflowers in my yard grew taller in a patch out back.

The rabbits hid there like the geniuses they are at laying low.
Another day, today a day of blue skies. Unpredictable.
Easier to remember than others. On all the new flowers, the centers
circle out further and further. The seeds grow bigger.
Hundreds of edible and viable seeds filling the center up.
The petals are yellow as the sun, the sun is yellow as the petals.
Here in this way you become the same to me as you were back then
even as time has passed. You are exactly as you were,
unchanged. And the flowers I've drawn on the paper are for you.

And I know no matter what else happens in time the petals will
open up again, the way I imagine they must be, yellow as the sun.

WAY TO GO

It helps to have a liar in office,
it makes the citizens feel honest.
Opioids are useful, so are pints
of banana ice cream, so long as they come
from a pharmacy. Hypocrites have two souls:
one for what they say, for what they do, another.
(ditto for fraternal twins and multiple personalities)
You can't believe traffic signals or crosswalks these days.
It's why motorists run red lights, careen into those faithful
    pedestrians.
You could trust alternative facts: ethnic cleansing, enhanced
interrogation, extrajudicial killings, and pre-emptive strikes.
You could meet a person of interest someday. Start a family.

The disguise is so comfortable, you'll forget
that you're wearing it. The mask that grows right along with
    your face.
The decoy that forgets it's a decoy, paddling,
falling in line with the fuzzy yellow goslings, falling
madly in love with their mother, falling
right between the crosshairs of the rifle.

All the toys in the sex shop look like ordinary objects —
squirt gun, ham sandwich, gooseneck lamp, ironing board . . .

Oh, how was he to know?
He just wanted to be loved
and famous. No one told him

the cameras were rolling, that
the mic was still on.
No one ever said not to grope *those* women,
no, not in so many words.

Maybe he already knew that,
but of course, nature calls . . .
After all, our goal is procreation, survival—
in fact, nature could come to our rescue: avalanche,
thundersnow, clouds bursting like arteries. Deadly fork,
lightning strike, brutal pretzel obstructs windpipe.

He slowed traffic behind him to match her speed.

HOW THEY LEARN

It's for us to remember, the night of the Labor Day Fair, the one when Alaina was attacked. Here, in our town on the bank of the Illinois side of the Mississippi, this is what men like us tell one another near the end of a day, recounting what we know from memory, at gas station counters, or along the school breezeway waiting for evening conferences with our children's teachers, or when we pass one another along the side of the road, walking our dogs by the light of passing cars. We tell one another what we know to corroborate, to learn what we didn't yet know, because a shared pain is a softer one.

That evening, before the fair, the lights in our homes went dark as we flipped off our living room lamps and shut the front doors behind us. We followed our wives and children as they piled into the front and back seats of our trucks, cars, minivans. We drove, our hands at ten and two on the wheel, and we looked out the side windows at that sky going gray with early evening, with the fireflies already out, and at the glow of the large electric bulbs on the food and craft tents of the Madison Park fair and the woods around them, and pin oaks and magnolias shifting in cool wind of the late-summer night. With our children murmuring words we couldn't hear in our backseats, we could see the path, the one we had taken even when we were teenagers, that curves west to the levee, where from atop it the river can be seen, flowing sluggish and wide, and black as the sun sets. Up there, where we had squeezed young girls tight to us, until our hip bones kneaded hip bones. We looked out to the western bank, with its sparse orange street lights and rows of late-season corn stalks, not far but like an island off-shore, connected only by the thin, rusted railroad bridge, brutish and ugly as a spear.

God, what we wouldn't give to know them better, each of the kids in this town, boys who are our cooks, our car washers, camp counselors, trainees at the accounting firm. Our nephews and our sons, and the girls they seem to think they love. But love doesn't look like this — like Alaina, the way she is now, the way we imagine her to look while we pray each day for her to gain the confidence to take off the gauze that wraps her face.

That night, the teenagers circled around the tents, slipping between the periphery of the fair and the woods like night animals, reappearing in their clusters still carrying their mounds of cotton candy, and their bratwurst, and their oversized bags of half-eaten kettle corn paid for with the money from their part-time jobs. In the bleached light from the music stage, each looked self-conscious in their own way, with mustard lingering on a lower lip or hands stuffed into deep pockets. Yet from the dark we could hear those same kids howl and laugh and shriek, even over the music onstage and the drone of the crowd.

They were all too young to drink, but we would have let them that night if they had come back to us, as buzzed as we were, seated beside their mothers and their younger siblings at the food tables. We would have slid them a half-beer, followed by another full one, grinning negligently, slapping our hands on the table in rhythm to the old songs the cover band played, pretending they still sounded as good as when we first heard them. But the kids would pass on the beer that night, just like we would have at their age. Though we wouldn't say it, those Madison Park bushes in the dark rarely failed to bring us back to our own first times. Tugging at zippers, our own and the others, hot breath in our faces, the first touch of a breast with its nipple going hard beneath our cold thumbs. Our bare skin against the prickle of the ground, and their hair, soft with conditioner, on our thighs, with the kind wet of their tongues. We count our children's birthdays and think back to the age we were at these fairs, and cast it from our minds, knowing unconsciously not to squint when our eyes catch on something in the darkness.

Elizabeth from the post office was working the beer taps that evening in September, already wearing her Fraulein dress, her breasts framed in lace and her fingers dripping with the foam of beer. We remember Mary O'Leary knocking her drink over onto her husband, his food and his shirt sleeves. We remember Alaina, older than the other kids, come back from college after her father died, working the candle booth with her mother, bored and rolling a lit cinnamon spice back and forth on its bottom rim, her face alight with the glow. With the night growing darker, and the stars just starting to swim in the black lake of sky as we watched them, and our youngests falling asleep with their heads in their mothers' laps — even though the band still played, we knew it was time to leave. "They're high schoolers, they can drive each other home," we said to our wives and each other, laughing, and we pulled ourselves up, put children in our arms or on our backs, threw away our plastic plates and half-drunk beers, and headed out towards the street. The headlamps of those cars parked along the roadside alighting as their families filed in, and the thumping of closing doors, and Mary O'Leary's voice leaking from the cracks in their backseat window. "You don't fucking touch me like that," she said. "I'm your wife, and you don't grab me." And we kept walking on, eyes forward, as if those windows had been rolled up enough to seal her voice shut.

Alaina rode her bike from the fair that night, leaving to go across town to work her graveyard shift at the convenience store of the Kangaroo station. She was used to riding in the dark, we knew, but we gave her a wide berth in our cars, even though there was a bike lane. Our teenagers would be leaving soon, they texted us, and we imagined them getting into their own cars the way they did in the mornings before they left for school. In the driveways, adjusting mirrors, the seat backs erect so that even the girls' heads nearly grazed the ceiling. Their hands on the wheel, ten and two o'clock, the way we taught them in the parking lot behind the derelict movie theater.

At home we lay next to our wives in bed, looking at our phones, swiping through news stories, with the humidity from the corn and river thick even inside our homes so that our fingers left streaks across the screen. Thinking how in our town, we taught our kids the lessons we were taught, good fathers we were: the girls to be independent and smart and brave, and the boys those same things, and the importance of not letting those girls forget. There was no local news that night — our stories are rare and so slow to be reported. But when they were, we read them slow like students with textbooks, working through each word. We know each reporter here, and each of the players on Quincy High's basketball team. We know the street corners and the businesses when the news is made, and often we even know the owners of cars in highway accidents by only the model and color. This is our town, and what happens here is ours, those stories enough to stay with us always. That night we turned off our phones and our bedside lamps, slowly growing drowsy, hearing the revving of a car's engine outside, waiting to hear our front doors open and close, so we could go to sleep.

Not long ago, Amanda Marble, who runs her own contracting business, was in a bar fight in the Royale Pub on Seventh. A man we know put a knife beneath the clefts of her breasts and tried to get her to go out back with him. Amanda, this big grinning moose of a woman, wrecked that man. She got him on the floor and wedged the legs of a barstool into the gut below his ribcage. Still, she had her face and forearms cut, and afterward missed a week of work.

There was Heather Giselson at the Family Dollar, whose ex-husband came back while she was on her knees re-stocking dish soap in the aisles. By the time she had convinced him to leave he had broken three of her fingers.

There was Grace, now a senior at Quincy High School, whose mother came upstairs when her boyfriend was over. She opened Grace's bedroom door to find him holding her daughter against the dresser, slapping the girl's face.

From what we know of that night, and Alaina, we know from news reports, from Mrs. Hanely, who was there at the end, from what we know of this town, and from what we already know. Alaina would have pedaled from the park in the bike lane, avoiding the street detritus that was always there, the roofing tiles and broken glass. She would have ducked beneath the low-hanging pin oak branches planted along the sides of the streets, always so slow to be trimmed. There is only one traffic light between Madison Park and the gas station, the rest of the intersections stop signs, but she would have ridden through it even if it were red, slowing as we had seen her do before, leaning on her handlebars to check for oncoming traffic. The blocks are short, but the Missouri brick our grandfathers built with made a smooth face of the downtown storefronts, let her see nearly half the town when looking both ways.

There was traffic alongside her, the cars coming home from the Labor Day Fair, and she would have felt the breath of air pressure of each one as it passed. We imagine what she looked like to them, those boys driving: her bike seat low, so that her posture was erect and rigid; her hair in a ponytail, whipping; her backside on the seat, like a full heart; the profile of her face.

The first drove alongside her, passenger window rolling down, both hands on the steering wheel. He would have spoken each word like it carried the same weight.

"Hey, you're Alaina. I've got a big, fat cock."

He slowed traffic behind him to match her speed. He kept the car in the middle of its lane as if it were being pulled by a rope. "Did you hear me? I said I have a big, fat cock."

Alaina laughed at him, she told others later. She told him sure, okay, sure, and when he wouldn't leave she said to him how she didn't want him, or his broke-down Honda, no matter how fat that cock could possibly be. The very fattest chode. She told him all that, pedaling smooth alongside him, looking at him like she would a little boy, and she laughed.

Even in the dark she could see his face grow tight, see his

teeth when the lips pulled back to call her "Bitch, you bitch." His hands on the wheel, at ten and two, dipping to the right so that the car drove into the bike lane. Alaina swerved to the side, the bike ramming into the post office's curbside blue box, the momentum carrying her body off the seat and onto the bike's frame. She looked, but the boy had driven off and the car was gone.

Some have spent time wondering how a young man thinks that will work, about how why he thinks a woman will want to be spoken to by him like that. His expectations, warped pubescence, thinking about how — perhaps — the both of them will stop, in unison, pulling off to the side of the road to put her bike into his backseat, the two of them pushing and pulling together on either side of the vehicle so that the foot pedals don't catch on the seatback pockets or the cumbersome center console. And she'll ride to his home shotgun alongside him, or else direct him to her home, where they'll go in together through the backdoor to either his or to her room, where the bedside lamp would still be on, and would be left on while she loosened his belt. But we know better about them, the boys, and what they want. We know how they do know, or a part of them does, that those girls will never say yes. When they turn to her and open their mouths they know already each word to say.

The next car to pull up alongside Alaina was another boy, red SUV, alone, passenger-side window already down. He said to her how he saw the whole thing, what an asshole, was she okay. He stopped his car in the road and waited for Alaina to collect herself. We imagine the deep breath Alaina would have taken when she pulled herself back up on the bike seat, steered back onto the road. How she might have bitten her tongue when her bike rammed the blue box, so while she pedaled she would have sucked at the blood taste and pain. She was okay, Alaina said she told the boy. She was okay and thank you.

He drove slow alongside her, and the traffic behind them continued to collect, some cars passing when they had the chance. He told her how it was too dark to be biking out there, and how if he were her boyfriend she wouldn't have to. Alaina slowed for the stop sign, looking each way to see that the streets were empty, and continued on without stopping. His SUV crept through the intersection alongside her.

"Leave me alone," she said, and he told her he was joking and asked her to relax, and asked where she was going. Leave me alone, she said, leave me alone, and he rolled down his driver's side window and spat, leaning so far out the side of the car that even his shoulders disappeared from her sight. We know Alaina pulled over onto the sidewalk when his car drifted into where she had ridden a moment earlier. We know that when he pressed on his brakes, he turned in his seat and pursed his lips and looked at her, hard. We know his tires squealed when he pulled away.

After that we figure she would have biked on the sidewalk for a few blocks, until it ended, until she would have pulled once again back onto the road. The row of cars that had built behind her would loosen, and thin, and dissipate, and she would watch their red taillights slow at the intersections ahead and turn off, right or left, out of sight. Perhaps the porch lights of houses would be going dark just before she passed them. When the bike lane disappeared, she would have ridden just alongside the curb, and she would have seen a car passing in the intersection in front of her, hardly stopping for the sign. There would have been the revving of an engine beneath the rustling of leaves in the breeze. There would have been a moment of recognition, like a sudden emptiness, in the moment the first car again pulled up alongside her.

We don't know how they're learning what they are, the boys in this town. How could so much for them be the same, but they grew to be so different? The same streets and storefronts as when we were boys. The same schools, with the teachers now grown gray, science labs with brown corroded beakers and scalded table tops, and the same gym, with the paint of its blue bleachers chipping, refurbished, and now aged and coming loose again. The trails through the Madison Park woods to the levee, and the same last names, so many faces so similar to the ones we remembered as kids.

And then, we were different, or else we grew to be different. There are those memories we do well to forget, or do our best to remember different than how we know them to be. At night, when holding our wives' breasts in our hands, thinking before sleep that, in some way, we are good men and good fathers, those memories come back, not quite surfacing, gentle like the sound of a doorknob turning, the ones that make us think: except. Memories of those girls lying on our small, twin beds beneath our bodies, or in the cramped back seats of our cars, or in the dark on the ground beside the back patio of our friend's home, where the music of the party inside could be heard along with the passing of the cars on the street—the girls being asked the question, that question, and saying yes, or something like yes, not yes, or nothing at all, and the answer to us not meaning a thing. Those girls we grabbed, or sometimes more, when they were yelling at us, or us at them, and though we don't remember exactly what we did or how we did it to them, we remember their faces after. We remember their mouths, half-open and breathing heavy, and their lower teeth. Their mouths, and the eyes we did not see or did not want to see. These are the women who are our wives, or our friends' wives now, or else they're gone, left town, or passed away. They're in the other room, where the kitchen plates are clinking, or in the bathrooms, or in their offices, the doors closed with their soft music playing. We don't know how they see us, or continue to see us, or how they don't see us very well at all.

When the boy in that first car returned to Alaina that night, he pulled up and he asked her if she remembered him. He didn't wait for an answer. He had it out already in his hand. He threw the liquid, from a worn glass beaker, across the passenger seat out the window and into her face. Hydrochloric acid. He wanted her to live. How does a boy even get that—here, in Illinois, with nothing but the river and the farmland outside the city for miles, lakes and interstate hours and fields of corn and soybeans with only unmanned irrigation systems and tractors slow in the distance? It's not ours, we want to say, that's not a thing we do here. It isn't ours. Because we wouldn't have used a thing like that, when we were that age, we wouldn't have done that, because we didn't have it when we were that age — but if we did?

He put it on her face, on the soft swell of her cheek so that it was stripped to raw tendon; her ear, so that the lobe pulled up and back and was only yellow cartilage; her nose, never delicate, but now shrinking, uneven; her brown eye, with the chemical between its lids, too far gone, what remained of it to be cut out that next evening by the surgeons. We think of Alaina's face in parts, because we can't comprehend it as a whole. We don't think of the pain.

It was Mrs. Hanely who drove her Civic up onto the curb, bursting its front right tire, who cradled that girl's grown body in her arms, and carried her full weight into the car, and drove her to the hospital, the flat tire thumping, speeding through each traffic light. Alaina's face in her lap, Alaina chewing into her thigh, and later, much later, in the white quiet of the emergency room waiting area, the burns Mrs. Hanely realized she herself had suffered from Alaina's face pressing against her, the streaks of raw red flesh across her legs.

Some lessons we worry aren't even taught by our words or what we do. We worry some lessons are taught by our eyes, from the blood pumping in our veins, from the look of our face, from the pores in our skin. We worry they learn from our hands even when we sit in the dark, on the edge of our youngests' bed, reaching to touch their neck as they sleep.

We go back to our own beds, and there they look at us always with forgiveness. In their minds, we're all separate. They look at us like we've never hurt a thing in all our lives.

THERE IS ONLY NOW

"We are told to accept what is happening to us because of ancestors wrong doing, but it is all based on historical lies, exaggerations and myths." –Dylann Roof

Nothing happened.
I was there.
I was not there.
The body swung like a pitchfork.
The bodies hung like lanterns
from the bridge.
Their mouths were stuffed
with rags.

This never happened.
This still happens
every time I cross the bridge,
black bodies swaying
above the water,
white bodies crowding
on the bridge,
looking down to see.

Am I more afraid
of a corpse or my shadow,
my shadow or my hands,
the blind spot,
the rope creaking,

and those white bodies
looking down:
their faces blurred
against the background
like ghosts.

Laura Sweeney

BEFORE I KNEW OUR FUTURE

It was August, at the retreat in Grin City
and I said your eyes are your best feature.
Blue, like the scarf I wore the night we
got together at the Voodoo Lounge
like the water in the courtyard pool

like my favorite shirt on you.
You looked so good in blue. Not
red like your Cavalier or the berries
on the panna cotta. Not butterscotch
your favorite pudding or our mini-doxie.

Blue, like the rosary you gave me,
like the tissue paper it was wrapped in.
Not Cerulean, the poem we taught to
middle schoolers. Not Rainbow, the poem
you dedicated to me. Not psychedelic

like the O'Hare airport or *Across the Universe*
the movie that wooed me. Not white, like
the towel you wrapped around my naked body
when you served Kahlua and cream. Not silver
like the infinity ring. Not turquoise, like the earrings.

Not black, like your gloved hand that dropped mine
when I suspected something was happening
looking for clues everywhere but in your blues.
Like the cover of the *Anna Karenina* book you
slid towards me. You suspected something too.

It was easy to imagine teenagers from local towns coming here for late night parties with booze stolen from their parents' liquor cabinets.

THREE TIMES TO CENTRALIA

That Saturday in 1981 when 12-year-old Todd Domboski ran across his grandmother's backyard in Centralia, Pennsylvania, and slipped into a sinkhole, I was playing with my Princess Leia action figure, her hair pulled into tight round buns, laser gun tucked in her plastic hand.

Or maybe, I was counting my change, trying to figure out how much penny candy I could buy at the local store.

Or maybe, I was sitting in my bedroom, hiding my hands underneath my desk, counting my fingers to solve homework math problems and wishing I was doing anything else but multiplication.

The truth is I don't know what was happening in my life on that day. I would have been nine years old, and whatever I was doing, I was probably growing tired of the long rural Pennsylvania winters and waiting impatiently for summer vacation to arrive in my small hometown of Ridgway located in the northwestern part of the state.

Still, this much I know for sure: like most children, I was certainly unaware of the dangers of sinkholes. I knew about fires and floods, but what kind of force existed where the earth could split open and swallow a person whole?

My home, and thus my world, was sturdy. Yes, I may have felt the tremors of trains that rattled on the tracks by my home, or the mud slinking between my toes when I waded barefoot in one of the local swimming holes. Or I may have known, for mere seconds, the freedom of flight when I jumped from my backyard swing into the air before landing on the ground with a soft thud.

But I had no knowledge of how the earth could suddenly give

away beneath my feet.

I also was not aware of the drama unfolding in Todd Domboski's home of Centralia, a tiny town located right in the middle of anthracite country at the other side of the state. I grew up sheltered, rarely traveling more than 45 minutes anywhere, as most of what we needed was located in our small town. We never even went on family vacations, instead preferring to take day trips to Lake Erie or Pittsburgh. The state's coal history was taught to me not through the lens of an examination of coal mining labor, but instead, with explanations of the differences between bituminous and anthracite coal. Anthracite coal was a cleaner coal — harder to find, but a much better source of fuel; whereas, bituminous was a dirty type of coal and not nearly as efficient as anthracite. These descriptions always came down to one conclusion: anthracite coal, located on the other side of Pennsylvania, was valued, even though it was fast disappearing.

No one mentioned gas explosions or mine cave-ins. No one talked about Black Lung. No examination of the exploitation of child labor in coal mines was ever given. No attention was paid to the environmental dangers of coal mining.

I first visited Centralia through the pages of a book. Always attracted to works that are about my homestate, I was in my early 30s when I picked up *Those Who Favor Fire* by Lauren Wolk from a local library book sale. The novel takes place in fictional Belle Haven, a small town located in the eastern part of Pennsylvania. In the first few pages, I was quickly introduced to the main character of the story, who, like the rest of the town, was mourning the passing of another character, who had died when the "earth opened up and took her."

As a reader, I soon learned about this small town full of a strong sense of community. In one scene, the townspeople are decorating for Halloween, and while reading the author's descriptions, I was reminded of how my mother carved pumpkins with candle-lit toothy grins for our front porch. I was reminded of homemade costumes of superheroes, ghosts, and witches. I was reminded of going trick or treating door to door and eating homemade candied apples without fear of razor blades.

However, as I read on, I realized how different this small town was compared to my world, for in this story, parents were warning their children, not about the dangers of strangers, but of "the very ground they walked on." I was thrust into a landscape where people were, literally, living right on top of a fire. As the narrator in the novel explains, "Living on top of a fire makes people cautious. It makes them wonder whether a flaming tentacle is at this moment winding its way toward the root cellar. It makes them walk softly and sniff the air for sulfur, like a species of strange, two-legged deer. It makes them fight among themselves when the conversation turns to the tired old question, now nearly moot, of whether they should pack their bags and leave or stay, and quite possibly, die."

Although the setting in her novel is fictional, in one small paragraph, Wolk sums up the painful feelings of the real town of Centralia in the early 1980s. The "real" history of Centralia, at first, seems simple. At its peak, the coal mining town was home to about 2,761 people, a small, vibrant community, but much like other coal patch towns, the population struggled when coal ceased to be an important resource. Centralia was fast turning into another dying coal town in the eastern part of Pennsylvania.

Then, an underground mine fire that started in 1962 catapulted Centralia from being just another struggling small town to a national story that still makes news today.

Those who have researched Centralia's fires disagree about its origins. Some say its beginnings stemmed from a garbage fire; others believe that the seam that runs under Centralia was lit by nearby mine fires. What is known is that there were many efforts to extinguish the flames, but the fire spread and in the 1970s, concern grew for the safety of the residents, especially after high levels of toxic gases were measured in their homes.

And then, there were the dangers of sinkholes.

Sinkholes are caused when the ground collapses into an

empty space beneath the surface. Most of the time, sinkholes occur in karst terrain, a term used by geologists to explain the type of rock below land surface that can be dissolved, mostly by groundwater—or in the case of Centralia, by an underground burning coal seam that could eat away at the world beneath us.

Luckily, that February day back in 1981, Domboski managed to grab hold of a tree root and was pulled to safety by his cousin. However, his slide, and the subsequent picture taken afterwards, where he stands at a safe distance staring at the sinkhole that almost swallowed him, brought national attention to the dilemma facing those who lived in Centralia.

By 1984, according to Deryl B. Johnson, author of the book simply titled *Centralia*, an estimated 7 million dollars had already been spent extinguishing the fire with no success. Experts determined that the only option remaining to effectively battle the fire would be a massive trenching operation, at the cost of about $660 million, with no guarantee of success. Johnson further explained that because they were left with such limited options, the townspeople in 1983 voted to relocate—a process that cost the government about $42 million.

Relocation may be considered a fancy and political word for helping residents leave their homes. Some, however, would say that relocation is just another way of saying that the government forced Centralia residents from all they ever knew.

However the term is interpreted doesn't really matter because in the end, most, but not all, of the residents of Centralia left their homes.

"Whoever said you can't go home again must have been from Centralia," says Cate, the main character in Lisa Scottoline's mystery novel, *Dirty Blonde*. Cate may be a fictional figure, but her words ring true for those who grew up in Centralia and then moved away. Today, there is really no way to go home to Centralia, as what is left of this tiny town is mostly only cracked pieces of paved roads, old signs, and worn driveways that disappear into lots of overgrown brush and weeds. Some homes still stand, but not many, as most estimate that between 6 – 10 people still make this place their home. Centralia doesn't have an official zip code and it doesn't even exist on most maps. It would be the perfect example of a ghost town, except there really isn't any town.

What residents (both current and past) of Centralia call home is named many other things by many other people, as this non-town seems to be located everywhere from Internet sites and blogs to Pennsylvania history books.

It's a curiosity — open almost any travel guide that explores Pennsylvania and there are sure to be a few pages devoted to this town, including the *Weird USA* series edited by Mark Sceurman and Mark Moran.

It's also a popular culture image. Online Youtube videos abound with those who visit Centralia, video camera in hand hoping to catch a glimpse of flames and smoke from the famous fire. The horror movie *Silent Hill* gained inspiration from Centralia (or perhaps other towns like Centralia). There is even a comic book titled *Carbon Knight*, where a hero rises from the depths of a mine fire to save the universe. (Or at least eastern Pennsylvania!)

Besides Lauren Wolk, novelists Tawni O'Dell and Natalie S. Harnett also use Centralia-like settings in their books. In fact, in the very first chapter of Harnett's book, the young main character's aunt is killed in a sinkhole that opens up and gulps down her home, a tragedy that is eerily reminiscent of the very real sinkhole that tried to swallow Todd Domboski.

It's easy to see why Centralia's mine fire attracts so much attention. Photographs of Centralia often show an eerie fog-like smoke that slinks through the shallow woods that surround the town. There were even places where fire could be seen fingering its way through crevices in the earth and cracks in the road. Especially haunting are the images of St. Ignatius cemetery, which still stands off to one side of Centralia's crossroads.

In essence, Centralia is a ghost story, an environmental

warning, and a political commentary in one tale.

But it's really more.

And this is what I discovered when six years ago, I went to find Centralia.

Traveling to the eastern part of Pennsylvania is easy enough. From my home in Northern Pennsylvania near the New York state border, I drove an hour south and then got onto Route 80, which cut across the center part of the state. Four hours later, I entered anthracite coal country as I got off the exit for Bloomsburg.

Then, I discovered that finding Centralia is not that easy. I ended up relying on the kindness of strangers (locals who gave me a few directions) and a number of battered road signs, left over from another time that counted down the miles.

First, Centralia was seven miles away, and then it was five.

Then, I was a mere two miles away.

Then, I drove through a crossroads with little evidence of any town. The only way I could tell for sure that I had arrived at my destination was because there was a set of wooden benches sporting a heart-shaped sign saying, "I Love Centralia."

I pulled my car to the side of the road and parked where I saw signs warning me of the mine fire: "Walking or driving in the area could result in serious injury or even death."

But otherwise, there was no evidence of a world burning beneath me.

According to The Pennsylvania Department of Environmental Protection, there are about 38 known actively burning mine fires in the state. Only about one-third of these fires are in the anthracite region; the rest can be found in the bituminous areas.

I grew up in bituminous coal country. I never thought about fire beneath my feet unless I was listening to a Sunday school lesson that preached the perils of hell.

However, I had seen evidence of mining in the shorn hills by my friend Robin's home, and the effects of acid mine drainage that turned creeks orange and stained river stones and weeds strange colors of red.

So, that day in Centralia, as I crunched through dry leaves and weeds in an overgrown lot, I looked for indication of fire.

But I didn't even smell smoke.

Instead, I saw wooded hills cradling the crossroads in late afternoon shadows. I saw graffiti scrawled across broken streets and beer cans and cigarette butts thrown in the roadside gravel. I saw overgrown meadows of Queen Anne's lace and goldenrod. I saw patches of black-eyed Susans that seem to nod at me in the breeze. I saw a groundhog scamper across the road, and red-winged blackbirds and catbirds darting among the leaves of sumac bushes. The air smelled like something was burning, but it wasn't the harsh scent of sulfur. When I breathed in, all I could smell was autumn air.

It was easy to imagine teenagers from local towns coming here for late night parties with booze stolen from their parents' liquor cabinets. It was easy to imagine that at any moment, an old pickup truck would come rambling down the road, spewing blue exhaust. It was easy to imagine little kids walking along the side of the road, perhaps even a little girl, picking daisies to put in her hair.

As I looked around me, realizing the small-town life pictures I have painted in my head are sentimental, I could easily imagine a time when residents called this place home.

Canadian writer Margaret Atwood, in her essay "Approximate Homes," contemplates the reason why everyone always says "down home." She says, "I used to wonder—why was home always down? Nobody ever said up home. But now I know: home is down the way memory is down, and hidden springs of water. Derelict cities, abandoned bones, lost keys. Home is buried. You have to dig for it."

I pushed my nostalgic feelings aside. If former residents of Centralia came back digging for their home, indeed, they may only find the flames that for now, eluded the very landscape where I was standing.

It had been four years since my initial visit to Centralia, and when my partner and I traveled to the eastern part of the state to attend an Oktoberfest, we found ourselves driving through the anthracite back country of Pennsylvania. We drove through towns with overgrown yards pockmarked with political signs. "Trump digs coal" many proudly proclaimed, and Anthony mused out loud, "Does he really?" He was not necessarily bashing a specific Presidential candidate — he was suggesting something harsher: "Does anyone in power really care about this part of the world?"

This was before the surprise upset that would put Donald Trump, a man who until he started his campaign, was known for his stint as a star on reality television. He had made many regions of the United States, impoverished places that are often ignored by both Democrats and Republicans, as a focus of his campaign, promising to bring back jobs to regions that now only have sparse remnants of the past as any sort of clue of an area that once flourished. Indeed, his presidency has pushed these regions into the limelight and placed the residents in full, often unfavorable, views.

I know the critiques of these regions. Those who live outside Rust Belt rural counties and Appalachian landscapes are often dismissive, wondering how anyone could believe the glory of the past, whether it's coal mining jobs or industry that once offered families a weak, but some kind of financial security. "Pull yourself up by your bootstraps" is a common refrain of advice for people in these economically depressed areas, and ironically are spoken by the same people who are seemingly dismissive of rural poverty and more sympathetic to the urban poor.

So, perhaps this population saw some kind of savior in a man who at least appeared to listen to their needs.

Still, I knew better.

The question wasn't really "Does Donald Trump care?" The question was really, "Does anyone care?"

The answer then, as now, seemed to be no.

We drove through small town after small town after small town. Many of them look alike, with wide streets and businesses that somehow get the word coal into their signs, whether they are tattoo parlors or pizzerias. With the exception of an occasional Dollar General store located here or there, most of the towns do not have the typical chain restaurants that seem to litter all areas of America.

I would like to say these towns looked quaint and inviting, but I can't. Many of the towns had blocks upon blocks of empty buildings decorated only by faded real estate signs that suggested the futility of any hopeful sale. One town eerily had a number of buildings charred by fire. "Arson," I said out loud to Anthony. After all, what would be the one true option of getting rid of unwanted property around here?

Graffiti also decorated many of the deserted buildings and sidestreets. I saw the typical pictures of hearts and arrows with names proclaiming forever love. One message, however, made me almost stop the car. Deep blocked letters scrawled on a side of a building screamed, "This shit needs to stop." I thought of the overgrown lots, the roads chipped and pockmarked, the chipped boarded empty buildings, even the presidential campaign signs, and I wondered, *Exactly what shit is the message speaking about? The fires? The presidential campaigns? The empty store fronts and homes? Or just the overall sad decay of what used to be vibrant and lively communities?*

Perhaps directions on the Internet are better, because this time, I did not have any trouble finding Centralia. When we pulled into the crossroads, Anthony, who had not been with me on my original trip, seemed shocked at what was around us. "There's nothing here," he said.

I didn't know how to explain to him that social media stories about Centralia glamorize what was now left of this small town. He probably was picturing the old dusty landscapes of Western ghost towns, the stereotypes found on movie sets. Certainly, the hundreds of websites from those who explore and catalog their adventures here at Centralia make it sound like the landscape was all thick smoke and hot flames and ghosts of the past.

But the only spirits who are still here are those who have found some peace in the cemeteries that remain in Centralia. We stood wondering about the few families that refused to leave, their homes nestled in a corner of what used to be a bustling community. Outside of the homes, Centralia has one church, The Assumption of the Blessed Virgin Mary Church, overlooking what used to be the small coal patch of a town. The church still holds regular services every week.

We had picked a cold and rainy day for our trip, and patches of fog hung low across the fields and the roads. The signs that warned visitors of the underground fire were missing, and I wasn't surprised. I had read that such signs keep getting stolen for souvenirs. Still, when I looked around, it seemed that the only thing really different from my visit years before was the missing signs.

There have been no recent reports of actual flames. While some believe that the fire has burned itself out, most say that the fire has simply moved further underground. Underground coal fires, especially anthracite coal fires, are difficult to put out. Scientists estimate that Mount Wingen, (also named Burning Mountain) located over 100 miles north of Sydney, Australia, has been burning for over 5,000 years. The mountain was at first thought to be a volcano because of the way that it spewed smoke, but later investigation into the landscape revealed that a burning coal seam ran deep underneath it. The traditional story told about the beginnings of the mountain explain that a woman mourned her husband who did not come home from battle. She climbed the mountain wanting to die herself, but she turned into stone, with her tears turning into fire. The burning tears lit the mountain on fire.

Already, through the power of social media, stories are being told about Centralia. I wondered how long it would be before no one would be living here to tell their stories. I also wondered how long it would be before the natural world totally took over the old lots and dead end streets, so that there would be little to no physical trace of Centralia.

Staring at the sparse world around me, I thought of our trip here. I wondered about the presidential campaign. I wondered if I would make a similar road trip in a year or two, if I would see any real change.

I wondered about what truly defines home.

I wondered how long it would be before the underground mine fire that was smoldering beneath our feet would burn and spread and perhaps find its way again to the surface.

GAYLORD BREWER

FIRE ON THE MOUNTAIN

Who lit the blaze, for what harsh
   purpose? Smoke a ghostly breath
   exhaled across the sugar cane,

snuffing each blade. Smoke
   in smothering tendrils into the trees.
   Then the clouds, dark army,

descending. Clash or caress,
   and some acrid and shifting
   new creature born. Smoke, cloud,

world one believed one knew
   dissolves to gray, to nothing.
   The black vultures circling,

white tips of their great wings
   reaching for it, slicing through it.
   A score of others heavy

on branches, sullen, shivering.
   What would death reward them?
   And the solitary short-tailed hawk,

perched and abiding in its hunger,
   wide breast rising, falling? In
   the mist, the merciless head turns.

ECONOMICS

Yes, I have taken what I wanted
from this country. The trill of the thrush,
the purring of the dove. Taken
the weary grid of the city,
taken the bread of my host,
the nights and torrents of rain.
But I have given my currency, my custom,
my sweat to an unmapped trail.
Given my blood to the flies
and my pledge to a deaf and muted deity.

What I have taken I took fiercely,
without apology, and I defy you
to condemn me for what I have done.

"You're wearing Grandpa's shoes?"

WHEN WE WERE ALL ON FIRE

Though the sign to our town read *Cows, Colleges, & Contentment,* in the summer all we ever felt was bored. Boredom smelled like pot smoke, burnt tires, spilt beer. Boredom drove the Mexican boys, the ones whose parents worked long shifts at the window factory or the packing plant, to fish the river for carp, fat gray carp that they hauled out of the water and beat to death on the rocks. Boredom drove the local kids to jump off the Second Street bridge into the stinking river. You had to be pretty bored to make that seem like a good idea, but the summer I was thirteen I had jumped into the river on four separate occasions before my older sister Kathy took an interest in me.

It was the first summer I refused to play softball or enroll in daycamp, the first summer I was left to my own resources, and every summer day seemed as vast, as meaningless, as the sky. Before that summer my closest friend was a girl named Tammy, a chubby girl with a pan-flat face who loved to bully the younger kids in Sunday school and whose friendship I had accepted simply because I thought I needed a friend, but that summer I had grown bored with her, and I was looking for something—or someone—new to fill the gaping hours. So when I hauled myself out of the river that fourth time and saw Kathy there, sprawled on the riverbank with a cigarette in her mouth, when I saw her wave me over, I thought maybe I had found it.

"Nice jump," she said, squinting up to where I stood smelling of dead fish, water dripping off my denim cut-offs.

"What are you doing here?" I asked her, surprised to hear how happy I sounded.

Kathy heard it too. With one shoulder she shrugged. With the other hand she picked her pack of Lucky Strikes out of the grass and held it out to me. "Want one?"

And to both of our surprise, I did.

In the two years before that summer, when Kathy was in the first throes of teenage rebellion, things had been tense. Kathy never wanted to go on any family outing anymore, or if she did go, she'd scowl. She'd sneak off to smoke, she'd make sarcastic remarks. When we'd go out for dinner she'd send her food back three, four times, just to be annoying, and then she'd make for the bathroom and never come back. Sometimes we'd find her out in the parking lot smoking with the busboys. Sometimes we wouldn't find her at all, and we'd spend hours driving around looking for her, asking after her at gas stations and pizza joints, calling up her friends. Sometimes Mom would stay up all night waiting for her to come in, and then she'd waltz in as the sun was rising and just whisk past Mom and up to bed without a word. When she was like this, it was like the house was this living organism, like this skin around all of us, and we were the organs, and she was the cancer. Stepping in the door, I'd know if she was home or not just by the way the house felt.

But other times Mom and Dad and I made this fun little trio, and it was almost like I was an only child. "Kathy," Mom would say in the morning, standing there in her ratty blue robe, buttering toast for us, "we're thinking of going to a movie tonight. What do you say?" Her voice straining so hard to seem casual that I would actually wince, smiling at Kathy like her lips were made of glass, holding out a slice of wheat toast, and Kathy would just look at her, look at her like Mom didn't mean anything to her, and say, "Nope." Just like that: "Nope," and grab the toast and head out the door. And Mom would keep standing there, and you could tell it hurt her, but she'd just butter some more toast and smile at me and say, "Well, I bet my Leslie is up for a movie, aren't you?" And of course I'd say yes.

By the summer I was thirteen and Kathy was sixteen, we seemed to have established a balance: the three of us on one side and Kathy on the other. Mom stayed out of Kathy's way, and Kathy let up with the sarcasm and the sneers and sometimes she'd even deign to call and let Mom know she wasn't dead or anything. After that day at the river, though, alliances seemed to shift.

At first it was the occasional cigarette smoked in Kathy's bathroom, a trip to Randy's Pump 'n Munch where she used me as a beard while she stole 3.2 beer from the cooler in the back, an afternoon when we drove around and around Main Street looking for something to do, until by mid-July, I seemed to have become Kathy's permanent sidekick—her drink-fetcher, her cigarette-lighter, her excuse-maker, her lookout. I'm not sure what Mom made of it; maybe she thought I could pull Kathy back into the fold or something. I'm pretty sure Barker didn't like it, but what could he do. Barker was Kathy's boyfriend, but he seemed to know his hold on her was pretty loose. He would have been a nothing—an average boy with average hair, a townie through and through—if it wasn't for his broken nose. He had broken it the summer before in a fight with some college kid—I never did get the details—and it healed crookedly, off-center. It made him look a little mean, a little dangerous, and I think that's why Kathy noticed him at all.

Back in what we'd taken to calling Kathy's rebel years, when we'd drive around looking for her, I used to think Kathy was leading this wild life. I would think of words like *orgy* and *overdose* and get this shivery feeling, there in the backseat of the car, looking at the back of Mom's head, at Dad's eyes in the rearview mirror. Instead, Kathy and Barker had a routine. We'd show up at Barker's house, this big ramshackle farmhouse on the edge of town with peeling paint and a toilet full of flowers in the front yard, and we'd find him slouched in a greasy armchair on the front porch, shirtless, a sweating beer can in his hand. We'd smoke a joint, and then they'd go inside for a while and leave me out front. And I had my routine: I'd steal a beer (or two) out of the fridge Barker's dad kept on the porch and lie out on the grass and listen to the buzzing of my blood.

That makes it sound boring, but it wasn't, somehow. I mean, nothing they did gave me that shivery feeling that I used to get when I *imagined* what they were doing, and yet, at the time, it seemed like everything they did had this edge to it. Barker would put his hand on Kathy's thigh and even hours later it seemed like you could still see the outline of it. It was like that feeling you have when a plane lifts off, when you feel the tires leave the ground, when you almost don't believe it can leave the earth, and you feel so heavy in your chair, you feel the tremendous weight of each person, each carry-on, each little breath even, and then, all of a sudden, you're up, the plane's up, and anything's possible. Being with Kathy and Barker was like that.

Sometimes, instead of lying in the grass, I crept around to Barker's window. Squatting under the sill, I listened to Kathy's little sighs and Barker's soft grunts, to the springs of his childhood bed slack and squeaky, something loud and abrasive on the stereo. Sometimes I stood on an overturned bucket with my eye to the corner of the window. Kathy on her back, eyes wide, the muscles in Barker's white ass flexing, his face hidden in her long brown hair, her hands splayed open on the black sheets. I hated that image of her, Kathy without her little sneer, without her cigarette or her brazen stance.

Anyway, when they finally emerged from the house I'd be thick with alcohol, my hands flabby as three-day-old balloons, my grin sloppy as a dog's I'm so happy to see them, and they, loose and feeling powerful, feeling like they shared some important secret between them, would be willing to take on an apprentice, willing to take me out of the yard and into the world.

Sometimes we went over to this little metalhead's place, some crummy apartment in the basement of the old medical clinic that smelled like urine and stale smoke and fried onions. Everyone called him Durham because he was from Durham, North Carolina, and no one seemed to particularly like him, but he would always share his joints. So we'd go there, or over to Mike Swanson's and watch Barker play foosball for a while, or we'd go hang out at the college and fuck around in the empty dorm rooms and light fires in the dumpsters, stupid shit like that, but if it was hot we went to the arboretum. Everyone did.

The arb was supposed to be an educational park for the local college, all the trees and shrubs bearing little plaques with the plant's Latin and familiar names beside a sketch of the flower or the berries. Instead, it was where the local kids hung out. In the summer it got downright nasty out there. The river was already bad from the farm runoff and the factory pollution, but add garbage, used condoms, urine, vomit, plus mosquitoes and what-all else, and you've got yourself a mess. But parents didn't go there, and the cops didn't bother us, and the college wasn't in session, bringing professors out there on field trips, so why not. You could grow weed there. Some kids even went swimming.

Kathy and Barker and I would lug a stereo and a cooler deep in there and spread out under the trees. Actually, if you got a good spot, it wasn't so bad. It could be pleasant. We would lie back under the trees and listen to the sixteen-wheelers rumbling in and out of town on the highway that led to the capital.

And then one day we went to the arboretum and everything changed between us.

The afternoon had started out as usual. The usual kids, the usual heat, the usual intoxications. Barker lit up a joint, something new, strong stuff, and it burned in my throat, inflated my brain. I coughed twice and sank back onto the blanket.

Kathy laughed. "You know, Barker," she said, "I'm really proud of our little science experiment here. She's really coming along. In a month or so we'll hardly recognize the brat." She poked me in the ribs before flipping over onto her stomach.

"I am not," I said, "a science experiment." Even to me my voice sounded petulant. They had been more secretive lately, whispering to each other, sometimes disappearing for a whole afternoon, and it had me nervous, a feeling the weed only inflated. I yanked a handful of grass out of the earth in a feeble attempt to seem tougher.

"Whoa—down, boy, down," Barker said, smirking.

"Leave her be," said Kathy, her voice sleepy and thick from the drugs. "She's going through a little rebellious phase. She'll cool off. Hey," she said suddenly, "why don't you show her our little surprise."

"What surprise?" I said, feeling a little tick of jealousy in my throat.

"I don't know," Barker said. "You think she'll get it?"

"Get what?" I said.

Kathy raised herself up on an elbow and looked at me, her head cocked to the side like she was sizing up a problem. "Sure," she said, her voice less certain than I hoped it would be. "She's a smart kid. She'll get it."

Barker looked at me, shrugged, then stood and started up the path without looking back, and I scrambled up and ran to catch him.

He veered off from the path, pushing his way through weeds and shrubs and junk, drawing us deeper into the arboretum. Through the thin fabric of his t-shirt his shoulder blades seemed sharp. I imagined what it would be like for Kathy to touch them, to run her finger along the finely drawn edge of his bones. I had never been alone with Barker, not like this, and I felt oddly excited, despite the dumbing of the pot. Barker swatted away a hanging vine, and I could hear him mutter "Shit!" Overhead the sky glowed white through the leaves. Somewhere behind us I could hear splashing in the river, the faint laughter of boys.

Barker led me into a clearing, a circle maybe fifteen feet across, purple and yellow with dandelions and thistles. A tall oak stood at the far end. "See," he said, pointing to the tree. He was grinning, and his voice sounded somehow proud, as though he were revealing a piece of artwork he had made. I looked at the tree, and at first I couldn't understand what he was showing me. There was a noose in the tree, of thick, creamy rope. "What do you think?"

"A noose?" I asked. "That's the surprise?"

Barker seemed a bit crushed. He rubbed the sides of his crooked nose contemplatively and said, "Yeah," looking off at his handiwork. "Kathy and I hung it up there last week. What do you *think*?" He turned and looked at me with such seriousness I didn't know what to say.

Finally I said, "I don't know, Barker. What am I supposed to think?"

He looked at me for a moment, and it was like I had disappointed him, or insulted him, and then he plunged back into the woods. "Never mind," he said, his voice dismissive, detached.

"No. Wait. Barker," I said, stumbling through the brush to keep up, "what's the noose about? Come on, tell me."

He didn't answer. When we got back to Kathy, who lay there twirling bits of grass around her finger like rings, he flopped down beside her, and without looking at me said, "She didn't get it. I knew she wouldn't get it."

"Her loss," Kathy said, tossing her grass rings.

I didn't know what to do with myself then, whether to sit down or to take off toward home. I just stood there, puzzled, almost hating them, and even after Barker slid down beside Kathy, even after they told me to leave, even after they started fooling around on the blanket, I stood there, unable to move or speak, looking at the shape they made, the shape of the leaf shadows, bird shadows, my shadow, on them.

After the noose incident, Kathy invited me to hang around with her and Barker less and less. "Get your own friends," she said when I tried to invite myself along. It was as though I had broken some code, some bond.

Mom noticed too. She asked if Kathy and I had had a fight, and when I tried to explain the situation to her—explain it in the vaguest of terms, without the incriminating details, without the noose—she cleared the piles of folded laundry off the sofa and patted the seat beside her. I sat down.

"They're teenagers, you know," Mom said, pulling one of Kathy's t-shirts out of the basket and holding it up in front of her. She cocked her head to the side. "Do you know this band?" she asked me, studying the shirt, and I shrugged but she didn't see. "When I look at her shirt like this, she still seems so small." She folded it in the air into a neat square and dropped it onto the Kathy pile. "They do teenage stuff." She grabbed two more shirts out of the basket and handed one to me.

"But I'm thirteen. That's a teenager," I said, and to my shame it came out like I was begging. I fumbled the shirt into a square and added it to the pile.

"In a year or two you'll feel differently. I know I did." She gave me a look like she wanted to say something more, but then gave her head a little shake. She picked up the shirt I folded, shook it out, and refolded it.

I took to following them. What else was there to do? I followed her when she stole cigarettes from the display case at SuperValu, when she and Barker hung around outside the municipal liquor negotiating with older guys on the purchase of beer. I crouched outside Barker's window when they spent the afternoon inside, fucking and smoking pot. But as the summer grew on, I spent more and more time at the arboretum, with their noose.

Thinking back on it now, it seems a foolish gesture, a melodramatic symbol of teen angst, an easy act of rebellion. But then, I don't know anyone else who's ever hung a noose in a tree. What did it mean to them? I kept trying to puzzle that out. Why did Barker seem so proud of it? What did he and Kathy want me to "get"? I kept going back to it as though it could teach me something, or explain something to me, as though it was one of those perception games, and if I stared long enough I could turn the vase into a face, turn the noose into something. Sometimes I sat on the other side of the clearing. Sometimes I sat in the tree above it, looking down. Sometimes I brought a sandwich and stayed all day in the woods, just staring at it, watching it sway in the breeze, the noose always open as a cartoon mouth. It could be a scream, or a yawn. It could be about to tell me something. As the summer grew on, the rope frayed and faded. Every once in a while, Kathy and Barker would come around, and I would have to hide then. They'd come as though they just wanted to make sure it was still there, and they'd talk a little, though I was always too far away to hear them. Once, Barker even rolled a stump under it and helped Kathy up, and then he slipped the noose over her head, gently, as if he were putting a necklace or a medal around her neck. And Kathy just stood there, grinning like she was receiving an honor. Then she threw it off, and she and Barker sank back into the woods. But mostly it was me there, alone. And I can't even tell you what I did all those afternoons, what I thought about, but I can remember the sky, looking up at it through the leaves, clouds stretching and clumping and shuffling on, birds zipping after mosquitoes. I remember listening for sounds—car horns, river splashes, animal calls—as though they carried messages. I remember waiting.

Finally, in mid-August, I broke down and knocked on Kathy's door. She made me knock three times—me holding my ear to the door between knocks, listening for some sign—before I heard her say, "Fine," and I could open the door and let myself in.

The first thing out of my mouth was "What's up with your room?" and I almost smacked myself, sure she would kick me right out again. I couldn't help it, though. I always remembered Kathy as a slob—clothes everywhere, cakes of eyeshadow smashed into the carpet, walls covered in pictures ripped from magazines—so I was surprised to discover how bare it was now, nothing on the floor and nothing on the walls.

Kathy was slouching against her headboard, her bent knees propping up a magazine. She looked around the room and shrugged. "I got tired of Mom spying on me. She'd clean up after me just so she could pick my pockets and go through my drawers. If I don't have anything," she said, sweeping one hand before her to take in the kinked blinds at the window, the dresser that looked as if some sticker had been scratched off with a razor, "then there's nothing to find. Take my advice."

"I don't have anything to hide," I said. I meant for it to sound a little pathetic, so she would maybe take me back, give me something to hide, but instead it came out sounding like Mom, self-righteous, and I shoved my hands in my pockets in embarrassment.

"Bully for you," she said, and went back to her magazine, flicking the pages. "What do you want?"

"Nothing. I don't know. Just wanted to see you."

"Well, you're seeing me." Flick went another page, flick.

"C'mon, Kathy, I'm bored. Aren't you bored?"

"No." Flick. Flick. And then finally, mercifully, she stopped and threw the magazine on the floor. "Well sit down then, you're making me nervous," she said, and I couldn't help it, I broke into a smile and scrambled onto her bed.

"Fuck's up with those shoes?" she asked, eying me hard, mouth twisted into a little knot of skepticism.

I forgot I'd been wearing them, and for a second I twitched my feet as though I could hide them, but then shrugged. "They're Grandpa's," I said.

"You're wearing Grandpa's shoes?" she said, and I couldn't tell whether she thought it was disgusting or funny. I had found the shoes in a box in the basement. Mom had cleaned out Grandpa's house in the spring after he died, but hadn't gotten around to giving the stuff to Goodwill yet. My feet had grown two sizes that summer, and the shoes fit. I liked the look of them, black looped with white, eyelets in the leather. "Wingtips," Mom had called them. When she saw me in them she had opened her mouth to say something and a look passed over her face, but all she said was, "They're called wingtips."

"Don't you think they're cool?" I said, holding my legs out in front of me for the two of us to admire. I'd scuffed the leather a bit, but they were still striking. Over the next year I would wear those shoes down to nothing.

"I think you're weird," Kathy said, but she was smiling and nodding her head, as though being weird was a good thing, and that's when she brought up the party. "Barker's throwing it. A cousin of his, some older guy from out West, is going to be in town this Friday, and he thought a party would be cool. What do you think, think you're ready for a party?"

And I said I thought I was.

When we got to Barker's the party was already spilling out into the street. The night was sticky and warm, and outside on the porch people straddled the railing, sprawled on the steps, slouched in the armchair. One guy I recognized from school, a thug that drove a jacked-up pickup so tall that he used a stepstool to get into it, had positioned himself behind the keg, trying to trade beer for a glimpse of tits. "Cow," he called each girl who refused. "Fat cow."

"So this is the party?" I said to Kathy, but Kathy just rolled her eyes and pushed me up to the keg.

"Don't even, Todd," Kathy said, snatching the flimsy plastic cup out of his hand and chugging it back.

"What about mine?" I asked, but Kathy just raised her eyebrows at me and strode off into the house, leaving me standing there with Todd.

"Are you sure you should even be here?" Todd asked. He was a small guy who made it worse by wearing small clothes—tight shirts, tight jeans. You could see there just wasn't much to him. He licked his teeth at me, raised an eyebrow, and though I didn't want to, hardly even meant to, I was suddenly flattered, flirting.

"Later," I said, leaning close. "If you're lucky."

Todd snorted through his nose and shook his head, looked away and nodded at one of the guys coming up the steps, but then turned back to me and handed me a full cup, the foam lapping over the edge. "I'll remember that," he said, and I chugged the beer back.

And suddenly the world is present tense. I am here. Some moments are like that, reaping us in an endless loop of experience, without meaning, without the possibility of reflection. I am here, at a party, and I'm flirting, and I'm feeling like, I don't know, like things might change for me. I am aware, in that moment, of my new breasts, loose inside the shirt Kathy loaned me, aware of the scent of me—something too musky that Kathy sprayed on me. Aware, in other words, of my sex, like it's dangling around my neck, some gaudy charm. I carry it inside the house, where it introduces me to a guy with a pipe shaped like a penis. "Put it in your mouth," he says, and I do, and the smoke is hot and burns in my throat and I cough and he laughs, they all laugh, but it is good. "She can take one," they laugh, and it's true, I think to myself, I can, and smile. "I can," I tell them, "I want more." And this is funny to all of us, we are all laughing: me, the guy with the penis pipe, boys with bongs and girls with big hair and mouths ripe and smeared and all of us walking around with our parts on fire.

"We're all on fire," I tell a boy in a Black Sabbath t-shirt leaning against the fridge, and I think he understands.

"Damn straight," he says, and turns back to his friend.

"We're all on fire," I say again, mostly to myself, and watch the house burn around me.

There must have been something besides pot in the pipe I smoked, I understand this now, but at the time it simply seemed like I could see through to the heart of things. I could push past people and it seemed like my hands entered into them, that we were briefly connected. I glimpsed a boy's eye and something inside me was kissed open. I was handed things to drink and things to smoke and I accepted them all with the benevolence of a novice.

At some point the party's hands passed me off to her, to Kathy, the queen of the party. I am jostled down the basement stairs, putty, a puddle, and I hear her voice, its deep-throated hum, a voice I now associate with blues singers, with crossroads and jug whiskey, not this girl in a basement, laughing on a floral sofa that smells of Cheetos and cat piss. Barker is beside her, pulling on a bong, some music full of fake-sounding guitars and someone's dreadful screaming in the background. There are other people down here — it's full, really — but I don't see them. Just Kathy.

"Kathy," I say, my tongue thick with happiness, but she doesn't seem to hear. She is taking the bong from Barker and tucking it between her knees, she is bending forward, the lighter clicking in her hand. I love the sound the bong makes, its little bubble of applause, and forgetting I am still on the stairs, I take a step toward her and fall, sprawling, at her feet.

"Someone's having fun," Barker says, and I think, *yes, yes,* and there is laughing, some of it mine, none of it Kathy's. I reach for the bong, but she gives it away.

"Not cool, Les," she says. She sits back on the sofa, pulls up her feet. Out of my reach. "Not cool."

I am trying to defend myself, to sit up, but my head feels so heavy, my neck weak as a weed, and I have to sit and wait for the world to right itself.

"Kath, let up," Barker says. He holds out the bong to me, but Kathy grabs it.

"It'd be a waste," she says, and swallows the end.

I know I'm being insulted, I know Kathy's mad, but I don't know why. I think to try my line, the one that made the others laugh, but I can't remember what it is. "We're fire?" I try, but Kathy spoils her mouth, blows out the smoke in neat rings. We watch them rise and spread.

"You're fucked up," she says. Then she unfolds from the sofa, her limbs impossibly long, stretching over my head and straightening. "Barker," she says, "be right back. Watch her?" and she actually points at me, like I'm a dog, a baby, something needy. The bong smoke and cat piss are making my eyes burn, everything too close and too much, and with my head dropped low I smell the stink of me, musky and artificial.

"You're not going to be, like, sick or anything, are you?"

Barker asks. His face looks greasy, smeared. I shake my head, and he mutters, "Cool," and leans back into the sofa, his eyes closed. He's still holding the bong and it tips slightly, the bongwater dribbling out.

And then I am on the sofa beside him, I am pushing into his side, he smells like pot and pickles, his skin hot where it touches my arm. My breast is pressed against his arm and it forms the circle of my world, all I can notice, and I put my mouth to his ear and whisper, "Barker?" He makes a moaning sound and shifts so that his hand brushes my thigh. "Barker, why'd you hang the noose?"

He takes that intake of air people make before they speak, and I think *yes, yes*, but instead he just smiles, doesn't even turn his head, just smiles, and then Kathy is there, above me, saying, "Go home, Les."

Outside the night is clammy hot. It makes the garbage smell hang in the air, gives rings to the streetlights. In three weeks school will begin again, you can already feel the earth slipping toward fall, but tonight the tree frogs croon in the maples and the police sirens sing of summer. I have no idea what time it is. I have no idea where I am going until I realize, at some point, that I have been walking toward the arboretum, toward Kathy's noose, and this makes sense, so I continue. Walking feels good, I like the firm stamp of my feet upon the sidewalk, how solid I sound, my feet alive in a dead man's shoes, and I am stopped in the middle of a block, testing the sound of my foot, when the pickup truck stops.

At first I don't realize it is stopped for me, and I stomp again, until the voice in the truck says, "It's probably dead by now."

I look up, squint. "What is?"

"Whatever it is you're killing."

"It's my foot," I say.

"I'm sure it is," he says. It's a man. I can see him now, see the shine of a nose, the shape of a head. He's leaning toward the passenger side window. "Need a lift?" he asks.

"A lift?" I ask. I am already sweating, my skin electric.

"Yeah, a lift home."

His pickup truck looks black but is probably blue. Looks new. My heart clenches under my t-shirt and I feel naked and no one is out and I know I should not get in the truck, I'm not stupid, but I do. I do. I see my hand on the handle and the door swings wide and he is sitting there in the yellow light of the cab, and then I'm in.

An ad comes on the radio, something about cars, and he snaps it off. "Where to?" He asks this as though he is carving the words out of wood. He is making a point not to look at me, one hand on the bottom of the wheel, the other flat and still on the vinyl bench seat between us. I cannot tell how old he is, but the hand between us is hairy, veined, nearly twice the size of mine, and I can't stop staring at it.

I give him my address and he lifts that hand off the seat, slides the gearshift, and we are moving.

We don't talk. There is nothing to say anyway, and so I roll my window down and put my hand into the night air. We take the usual route to my house, pass the familiar places — McDonald's, Denny's, Randy's Pump 'n Munch — and I wave goodbye to them as I pass. I am going places, I think. The buzz is wearing off, and in its place comes this sense of Thereness. I don't know what else to call it. I am There, both here and outside of here, and it makes my mouth feel strange, makes me feel rinsed out. It's like I am standing on the edge of the ocean and the wave has just gone out, I can feel it pulling away the old sand, can see the water clawing at the shore, but the next one is there, curling up behind it. I am standing on the edge of something big, feeling the moment rush away from me, and waiting for the next one to hit. Goodbye, Dave's Motors. Goodbye, Elm Street.

The truck passes my house, and I watch it slip past — sad little brick ranch with its hopeful front light — and wait until we are two doors down, in front of the Morris', before I tell him we missed it.

"Should we back up?" he asks. His voice is husky. His smell swells inside the cab, swallowing me. He takes a hand off the steering wheel and puts it back on the seat between us.

"Looks like it," I say, my voice nearly a whisper, but he just pulls over to the curb and puts it in Park with his left hand, awkwardly, still keeping his right hand between us.

There are lights on in the Morris' house. I've been in there before, took care of their pugs and brought in the mail when they went down to Florida two years ago. *They're in there now*, I think, *and they don't even know I'm out here.* Out there people are emptying dishwashers and tucking in their children and arguing in the blue glow of television sets. *I will never be one of them*, I think, and I don't know if I am pitying myself or them. The man at the wheel moves his hand up my thigh—slowly, tentatively, as though I might bolt like a wild animal, but I don't. Inside my body, at the core of me, things are heating up, switches are being thrown, but I don't move. When his hand reaches my crotch, when it inches, spider-like, into the crevice between my thighs, I grab it. He jolts, but I don't let go. I press it down. His hand is hot, the veins under my fingers thin and pliant, and I think *ropes*, and then I stop thinking.

A noose is a hole that needs filling. It's a gap, a loss. Once I put it around my neck and stood there a long afternoon. Once I thought about cutting it down and carrying it around with me, in my backpack or something, but I didn't. Then one day at the end of summer it was gone. Kathy figured the college groundskeepers cut it down. "Wouldn't want to give the little freshmen any ideas," she said when I asked her, blowing out a smoke ring and putting her finger through it.

Fifteen years from this moment I will hardly know Kathy. She'll still be living in our hometown, married to a guy who wears sport coats and has an invention for rock urns in their basement, patent pending. She will seem happier than I believe people are. I will be between jobs, between relationships, between cities. I will be in training for whatever comes next.

"Why did you put up that noose?" I asked her over the phone recently, and I was surprised to find it took a bit of prodding to make her even remember it.

"Probably just something to do," she said, "some idea of Brad's."

"Brad?"

"Brad Barker. You remember Brad. Nice kid. Good boyfriend." Her voice sounded so certain, complete, as if those years could be summarized so easily: nice, good.

"You always called him Barker back then."

"Oh god, don't remind me," she said, laughing, dismissive. "Did you know Brad lives in Denver now? He flies for one of the airlines, I forget which."

"But the noose," I said, and felt awkward and embarrassed even as I persisted. "I don't know, it seems like it must have meant something."

"Probably, but I honestly can't remember, Les. Why?" But I didn't have an answer for her, and she was off talking about something new, and the gap between us again swung wide.

KERRY JAMES EVANS

THE CENTURY HOUSE ON DEVONSHIRE

looked like the second coming —
white house on a hill
busting out onto the curb
like a proud mother
about to tell the same story she always tells,
but *You haven't heard this before!*
Still, we wanted it,
prequalification letter
folded neatly in my blazer,
church bells echoing off the glow
of dusk light draping a cedar,
porch wrapped like a farmer's belt
around a couple of big bay windows,
and damn if it wasn't perfect,
hardwood, clean lines,
ceiling that made me
want to reach. I walked up
the staircase, entered the master suite,
and when I got a look at the tub
I nearly stripped down
and hopped in. Then I heard
You might want to come down here!
Down I went, descending
what was more ladder
than stairs, down into the basement,
where cinderblocks crumbled
behind asbestos, green paint

I'm sure looked cheerful
before the water set in,
cracks running wall to wall,
support beams splintered
down the middle, and the door
leading outside? Wouldn't open.
Still, I tried. I tipped over a bucket
and tried to work it out,
filling the seams, replacing
the beams, telling myself,
We can make this work.
I said it knowing it never would.

SNOW IN SPRING

First a straight-down rain and then great
fists of flakes erase it all — the tender shoots

and tiny flowers, the daffodils that napped
in morning sun only yesterday.

Gone is the sky altogether, with its promise
of blue and the river, lost behind pale sheets.

Only the ground does not betray us. Under the skirt
of a holly, its limbs retracted by the weight

of all that white, a small circle of ground still
winks brown, a warm core melting

whatever snow shakes through as branches
tumble. And they drop across the landscape.

Old pines cracking like a shotgun blast, small trees
hooded and brought to ground, whole hedges

bent in half to reveal the neighbor's house, previously
screened by green.

Into this hostile beauty I plunge — wielding
an old broom, half its bristles gone, the others

blunted in a permanent curve — to beat those branches
I can reach, shake off winter's final crush.

I swing the broom like a drunkard in a barroom brawl,
all false bravado and empty punches. A fight I expect

to lose. More fury in every jab for just that reason.

It got in his beard, but he didn't care
and let it sit on his tongue.

PREDATORS

They crouch in the dry brush in the shadow of pine trees. David holds a rifle, not yet raised to aim because Michael has told him to wait. Told him with a firm squeeze of his arm that is at once a reassurance — you got this — and a gesture of love. It is cold in the shadows, could be October. The light is right, the days shrinking, but it's hard to know for sure. Their calendars are out of date, their memories scoured by days of repetition. Michael had said the rut happened in September, but it could be October.

David hears the elk bugle again. It's in the trees across the clearing of pale yellow and Michael has stirred its lust, its violence, with a whistling bugle that's a good imitation. Closer now. Can see its shape through the trees, antlers catching light. Maybe a trophy, but who cares about trophies anymore? Certainly not Michael, rail thin with beard and hair grown over a face bent into a scowl that could become a growl if the mood is right. Certainly not David, even thinner with a patchy beard of his own. They're both sick of their diet of rabbit meat supplemented by cornmeal, canned vegetables, and once watercress that tasted like mud.

Michael told him elk tasted good. Described the steaks his mother used to make from the carcasses he and his father brought back from hunting trips in mountains not too much different from these. That was Michael's childhood — hunting or fishing trips to woods by lakeside or on timbered ridges to hunt and hang deer by fire, dump your coffee dregs into fire come morning. He's a fine companion for the apocalypse.

The bull clears the trees and, for the first time, David gets a good look at him. A lighter coat than he expected, but dark head and antlers that are swept back in a thorny crown. He raises the rifle, striking a pose he never imagined in that long ago time when he lived in a city of concrete, cars, and order. David lines up on the elk, which continues its approach. He stares down the barrel at the animal that is looking for its rival, head sweeping back and forth. He knows that the elk will turn broadside and then it will be his chance at a clean shot. He knows that he should shoot and be glad for the bounty. He knows, but David freezes.

He sees the child's face again. A girl, her blue eyes big, innocent, and empty. She stared at him, a tiny head impaled on a fence. Stared and struck him so that he faltered, unable to look away even as Michael was telling him to run and there was a shot and a shout from the house. Run, but in that gaze were days of fire, looting, and gunfire in the streets. In those eyes were the ruins and the dead swinging from burnt carcasses of trees. The hiding, feeling hunted, and what was the point anymore? Run, but he didn't want to.

"David," Michael says. The rifle is unsteady in his hands.

"I can't," he says.

"Yes you can. Do it."

"I can't."

Michael reaches for the gun. He was quick on that night too. Saved David's life. Now he grabs the rifle and it goes off. The recoil hits David and knocks him back. The elk spooks, heads back for the trees. Michael stands, aims, shoots.

"Fuck," he says and then he is running.

David sits there, still dazed and thinking about blue eyes, blue. Michael disappears into the trees at a fast pace. David stands and picks up their other rifle and a pack they scrounged someplace. He knows Michael will not slow down in his chase. He runs after him.

Michael won't slow down, but running up a ridge winds David and he stops to catch his breath. He's looked for blood, a sign that Michael at least wounded the elk, but has not seen any. A breeze picks up as the afternoon lengthens into evening. It makes him shiver beneath the ragged flannel shirt he salvaged from a house along the way. David feels exposed being alone, but having the rifle helps. They've been alone for a long time now, but you never know.

"When you've given up expecting them, they will come," Michael often says.

David traces the crest of the rocky ridge, looking for Michael. One of the many rolling, timbered hills that lead off to high peaks he can see off in the distance. The mountains are covered in snow already. They stand out sharp and white in the distance. No sign of Michael, so he decides to pick his way down, keep going.

Bend knees, go sideways, David kicks his feet into the steep slope. He has never gotten over the fear of falling, that shaking in knees that says this is not natural, give me level ground. Careful, put feet on rocks, on roots, anything that resembles a step. Hear raven croak and wind in the pines, but eyes down on the slope in front of you. Be careful of the loose rocks that slip and —

David's left foot slips and he falls back. His right knee bends and his back lands hard. David slides on the loose rock he should have avoided and then he hits rock, root, and straddles a stump that slows him, but his left leg hurts. A cutting pain. He looks down to see a splintered root from the stump has punctured his leg. Blood. He lies there, afraid to move.

"Michael," he calls. Hears the raven, the wind.

The gun has slid further down the slope and is out of reach. David has long feared an injury like this. He has worried about cutting himself while skinning a rabbit, has run his tongue over his molars, imagining a dull ache that would grow into a jaw-splitting pain. No way to numb it. Even the alcohol is gone. Michael knows some basic first aid, David even less, but this injury looks beyond the skill of either of them.

His leg throbs. He shifts his right leg, which is still bent and sore, though nothing like his left. David wonders if pulling the root free is a mistake, if it will release all of his blood until he's left there, dead and alone. A tentative pull proves that anyway it will be painful.

As he falls back onto the rocky slope, David feels watched. He jerks his head around and sees a dark shape above him. It moves and he makes out a canine shape, black, watching him. He thinks dog, but it is large. He thinks coyote, but again the size and the color's wrong. He thinks wolf.

David scrambles now, jerk of pain that stops breath short as he lunges for the gun. The root pulls free of his leg and he shouts a wordless curse. Wheels back to level gun at wolf to find that wolf is gone. If that's what it is. The slope is bare again. David pants. He fires the rifle into the air.

"Michael," he yells with what breath he can muster. He pleads.

They live in a house on a hill that has a good view and views are good in this, what would once have been called "the end times." The words feel lame coming out of David's mouth, end times, and he avoids saying them. Avoids stepping in the traps set by memory of a life in that city living together in a nice apartment with wood floors and windows looking out on a street of red brick buildings, historical, desirable neighborhood with bars, restaurants, coffee shops. Everything a young man in his twenties could want. Get bogged down in remembering and you fall in the pit of depression and that means no snaring rabbits, no getting food to stay alive, no vigilance from that house on the hill that looks out over the valley on one side and the rolling timbered hills that climb up to mountains on the other. Michael had to help him walk over those hills after his fall, his leg tied tight to a makeshift splint, the pants stained with blood. Had to carry him up the last hill when the pain got too bad and David shook with it.

The house has stone counters and big windows. Wood floors and two stories the woodstove they set up in the kitchen can't heat come winter. A fancy second home for absentee owners. Wonder how far they got, if they tried to come here. Maybe the car broke down on that rutted, pothole highway strewn with burned wrecks and they were killed and scalped somewhere down the line or else enslaved in some wannabe warlord's harem. Best not to imagine.

It's a comfortable place to hide out and wait for—spring? The best you can hope for.

Even though they cannot use all the rooms, David likes the homey comfort the large house provides. After a series of burned out houses and rustic cabins—one with traps dangling from the walls like jaws of death—the water that still runs from a well is a luxury. Michael was nervous about its location on a bare hill, but he relented when he saw how much it meant to David.

David's favorite room is the bathroom with the tub and large mirror. He likes to take the occasional bath with water boiled on the gas stove, pouring it over his pale, naked body and using a disappearing bar of soap. Michael thinks this is a waste of time and effort, not to mention fuel, but David likes to feel clean, even if it's not as clean as clean used to be when he had a shower, a loofa, and chemical-free body wash. He says that Michael smells gamy, remembers holding him close and looking at the two of them in the mirror not long after they'd arrived and took a bath together.

"We look like Civil War soldiers," he said to the bearded, hollow-eyed figures.

"No," Michael said. "Biblical."

David lies on the mattress in the kitchen. He sweats, stripped down to boxers, under blankets with fire burning close by. His lips are cracked, never enough water, and his leg aches in the way it always aches now. He watches Michael skin a rabbit, his hands covered in blood.

Michael knows all this, grew up with it. From a small town and his camo-wearing father was what they used to call a redneck. As things are now, David envies his experience, though he's learning. David's whole life was spent in suburbs and city, with parents both dead long before it came time to flee. Maybe Michael envies David the orphan. Wonder if he ever thinks about parents—quiet mother and hard-jawed father David only met once on an ill-fated trip to let them know who their son really was, which ended with Michael's father shouting faggot and pushing Michael off the porch as David watched from the car. Wonder if he ever thinks about that, if they made it.

A wind rattles the windows. Always windy up here. But tonight there's a different note sown into that wind. It's mourning and it makes David feel sad and scared. A howling different than coyotes' yip-yip wail. Michael opens the door wide to let in cold air that pools around them as he looks out into the darkness and listens to the chorus coming from the hills. No telling the distance, but the source is clear. Wolves.

"Cool," Michael says.

"It's cold," David says. "Shut the door."

Michael has been skeptical about David's wolf sighting, but now he is enthusiastic about their return. His eyes fill with the light that is a part of what David loves about him. Back in the city, back in time, he got excited about a movie, a book, or a band and he would tell David all about it, the words coming all strung together and mixed with praise. He'd go on until David would laugh, kiss him, and say, "Yes, isn't it grand?"

Michael comes back one day to report that he's seen a wolf pack, bigger than expected and seeming unconcerned as they loped across a clearing. He watched them through his binoculars and noticed blood on their muzzles and chests. He tells David that he found their kill, an elk carcass dismembered and covered with ravens.

"Picked pretty clean," Michael says. "I half hoped for meat."

"Seriously? You'd eat what they left?"

"Why not? So long as it's not spoiled."

David can't tell if Michael is kidding. He's always had a strange sense of humor. Maybe less so now, but before he could find humor in the oddest places.

Michael has been telling David about wolves. He talks about how they will make prey—elk, caribou, bison—run while the wolves trot and look for weakness. Attack the old, the sick, the young, and the weak. Easier to bring down and when you're trying to survive, when all your energy is precious and not to be spent idly, easier is best. Michael talks about their social structure with a dominant pair, the way they communicate, and take care of one another as a family. He praises their resilience.

"Isn't it amazing they've come back here?" Michael says, taking off his binoculars and coming over to the stove, where it's warmer.

"You're not worried?"

"About what? They won't bother with us."

"Sure, but they eat deer and elk."

"Not enough to starve us. Might make it harder, but no, it'll be fine."

David goes back to mending the tear in his pants. All he has strength for now with the leg slow to heal. He's clumsy at sewing and pokes himself with the needle. Bead of blood that he watches grow.

"My grandfather would've trapped them," Michael says. His voice has drained of the enthusiasm that sparked in it when he came inside. David knows his grandfather owned a small ranch that was lost before Michael's father was five.

"And your dad?" David asks and knows he has made a mistake because Michael gives him that look, the one that you'd expect to accompany a growl.

"Him too."

Michael moves away from the stove to look out the window over the sink. David stares at the back of his head, the hair pressed down from his hat, long and curling down over his neck. He sees the bald patch that has been expanding in the last few years.

"What will you do?" he asks and it's quiet, like maybe he doesn't want an answer because he means to ask if Michael will trap the wolves but also in a broader way, what will he do? So many of their days now are Michael leaving, David waiting for him to come back, to bring him food. David feels like a baby bird, a helpless mouth gaping from a nest. If someone came, he'd be unable to fly.

"I kept the ivories," Michael says. He reaches a hand into

his pocket and pulls out two bulky teeth. Sets them on the table. David looks at them.

"Elk have some teeth called ivories," Michael says. "I'll make a necklace or something."

"Earrings," David says. "You only have two."

"I'll get more."

Days pass without meaning much. Sometimes Michael fails to get a rabbit and they go without meat. These dinners consist of dry cornbread, canned green beans. No more butter, but there is a crystallized jar of honey that David revives every now and then to add some taste to the bread that crumbles into sand in his mouth. Hungry. One day, he takes a bath and looks at his body — skeletal ribs and sharp hipbones. The wound on his leg oozes blood and pus into the pooled water. Can't be a good sign.

Snow falls in lazy flakes that remain suspended in the chilly air, a hallucination of snow. Michael says deeper snow will make it easier to hunt big game like deer and elk — slows them down. He never returns with game, but every night it seems like the wolves are howling and howling means a hunt, a kill, something. No words in that sad song.

In the cold kitchen, David shivers. Blanket on shoulders and fire burning, but still he shivers. He feels sick — how many days? Sick, shivering, leg throbbing, and sometimes Michael is there when he wakes in the night, a solid body wrapped around his, and other times he is gone and a weak, gray light shines on the curtains. David remembers their last can of fruit — peaches. Remembers punching a hole in the lid and drinking the sweet syrup that poured out. It got in his beard, but he didn't care and let it sit on his tongue, that sweetness, almost not wanting to swallow and have it be gone. He remembers the soft, slimy slices. He cannot remember when. How long? He cannot remember.

Michael is back, tending the fire. David watches him from the bed through heavy-lidded eyes. He feels as though he has been asleep for a long time, years in which the past has been buried in ash-like snow. In the room, it seems like night, but day and night have ceased to be different. He thinks he hears howling, but then it could be the wind.

"Do you ever wish you didn't have to come back here?" David says to Michael's profile.

"Of course not."

"To be alone." David watches Michael's hunched figure as a silhouette move around the kitchen. He pictures him as a lone figure out in the wilderness, a fur coat matted and smelling animal. David tries to sit up, but has such little strength.

"Here," Michael says. He pulls David up so he can lean against the wall—extra squeeze of shoulders and kiss on brow—and hands him a steaming bowl. Hunks of grayish meat in a weak broth, carrots. David pokes at the stew with a spoon.

"Is this—wolf meat?" he asks and the question sounds ridiculous in the stuffy room.

"Jesus, no. Elk," Michael says. He is eating at the table.

"I mean, is it from a carcass that they killed?"

"You don't think I could get one on my own?"

"Did you save the ivory?"

"Because I've done it before, you know. Got my first bull when I was thirteen."

"Before," David says. "When all was well."

"You're sick and not making sense. Eat up."

David stirs the bowl, brings a piece of meat up to his mouth, and holds it there. Feel the warmth, the texture that is like his tongue, but is not his tongue. So different than stringy rabbit. Not gamy, like tender steak. He swallows it. Anything can start to taste gross if you hold it in your mouth too long.

The fire cracks as they eat. Quiet kitchen with spoons clinking on ceramic bowls. This could be any time. It could be the end of time. All there could be is this room with its shrunken candles and stone counters covered in dust they no longer clean. Useless stove, oven, useless light bulbs in fixtures and maybe the switches have been left on and they wouldn't know.

David watches Michael's jaws move as he chews. Beard moves. It's so tangled and unruly, random curls crawling down his neck. Beyond the scruff that was once so fashionable. He has a starved, desperate look about him, David thinks. Bones moving in his face, working at the meat. Michael scratches, a quick, jerking motion. David wonders if he'll get fleas.

"Where do you go?" David says. "Days at a time."

"I've been hunting." Michael pauses to slurp stew. "Hard work with all this snow."

"Hard work," David mutters. While I just lie here, he thinks. "Is that right? I wouldn't know though, would I?"

"Why would you?" Michael says and shrugs.

"That's right. I'm just the dumbass city boy you happened to be fucking when the world ended."

"The world didn't end. It's still here."

"I think you like it, this whole macho mountain-man bullshit. You're getting back to the roots I tore you away from."

"You didn't do shit."

David can't eat anymore. The bowl sits in his lap. Michael finishes after waiting for — what? — and takes the bowl to the sink. The window there is covered in frost. He scratches at his long, greasy hair.

David wants to say something. He is remembering those conversations in their apartment, on the couch in front of TV or at the island in their kitchen. He is remembering how he told Michael his parents would still love him. Wouldn't it be better for them to know? Wouldn't they know him better? And Michael afraid in a way he hadn't seen before and wouldn't see again until there was gunfire in the streets and flames reflected in the mirror-like skyscrapers downtown and explosions that could be gas tanks or could be something else. Michael with his hunting rifle, the two of them with packs and sneaking through the streets at night, hoping not to run into anyone, hoping it wouldn't come to that. A series of images he never could've imagined pulling him away from everything he'd ever known. The past ran into itself and always ended with that child's face frozen in a question.

"The wolves work together," Michael says. He's still facing the window over the sink, but David thinks he must be watching him in its reflection. "I've been following them and watching how they do it. They have that dominant pair, the alphas, but they hunt as a pack."

"I'm tired of hearing about the wolves," David says. He is tired. In general. Feels himself slipping down the wall and hopes the soup won't spill.

"I'm saying it's better the two of us. Working together."

"What, you want me to help you more? Is that what this is about?"

"No," Michael says. He turns to face David, but he doesn't look at him. "I have thought about leaving."

"And going where?"

"I don't know. I just get this restless feeling, like I need to go. But I don't."

"Why?"

"It's better together. Isn't it?"

"I don't know. You're hardly here, even when you are."

"What would you do without me?"

"Is that a threat?"

"Jesus, I can't stand you sometimes. No. You'd be lost without me. Look at you! You can't even stand right now. And, I mean, if people came? Killing a man isn't the same as a rabbit, David. And no, you wouldn't know. It isn't even the same as killing an elk."

"I'm not ashamed of that," David says.

"It's this house," Michael says. "Cooped up in this one room like a cage and the air is so stale. It's different outside. The air is — clean." Michael pauses, finding the words. "Do you know what it's like to be out there, at evening, when the light goes blue?"

"You can leave if you want to," David says and he tries to sound bitter.

Wood sparks in the stove. The crack is loud inside the metal. Michael's eyes are downcast, his heavy lashes making it look as though they are closed, but David doesn't think so. In the low light, his face is dark. You could think that the whole thing is covered in hair the way it looks with its shadows. With two pinpricks of light for eyes and maybe the teeth showing where his mouth is. A featureless face covered in fur.

David's strength returns. It comes back gradually, a restlessness in his mind that spreads to arms and hands and legs. A morning and he can walk outside in the cold without feeling that cold go all the way through him. His breath fogs, he looks at the snow that is solid around their house, makes the pines look black on the hills that stretch on and on.

Michael must have shot an elk because he brought back meat stuffed in grocery bags, in backpacks. They work together, silent, in the kitchen. They cut the meat into strips, steaks, smaller pieces that are easier to work with. David salts some to save, but it is cold enough out they can pack it down in the snow on the house's north side for now.

Michael works at cutting the meat with a savage energy. He licks blood from his hands, from the knife. David isn't sure this is wise, but he doesn't say anything. He just watches Michael work, blood in his beard. The last words he heard Michael speak were that question he didn't have an answer to. Do you know? He didn't.

Maybe it's the meat, giving him strength, but David feels the wound healing. Takes a bath and it doesn't look so bad. He lies back in the lukewarm water turning cold and thinks about he and Michael swimming in a river in what must have been their first summer after leaving the city. First bath, if you could call it a bath, and their naked bodies pale in the dark hole they'd chosen for this swim. Diving and grasping at each other like otters. Michael said that—like otters. Lying on the rocks of that riverbank, they both relaxed. You could pretend it was only a vacation. You could pretend that nothing had changed. You could make love and not feel like that made you vulnerable out in the open where a stranger meant a threat.

Michael has stopped coming back to the house. Days pass, weeks, and David does not see him. The elk meat dwindles. Perhaps there was less than he thought, but David starts to think something is taking it. He looks in the snow for a sign and sees bird tracks, human tracks, but the boot prints must be his.

He cuts wood like Michael showed him, but his axe swings are uncertain and the blade glances off the logs too often. He quits after cutting less than he wanted to because he worries about another blow to the leg, getting cut. David sets traps close to the house for rabbits, eager to supplement the meager supply of elk meat, but rabbits stopped coming close to the house a long time ago. He takes his gun to search for food, for signs of Michael, but always keeps within sight of the house. Afraid that he'll miss Michael. Afraid that someone will take it from him.

There comes a night when a big moon lights up the snow as if it were day. David steps out into the cold that cuts his face and listens, but the night is still. Back into the room with the fire and a sleep that is full of padded feet running, claws click on wood floors and skid. Panting. You have to move, moving run. Skittering footsteps, clumsy across the house into the kitchen and David asleep. He wakes and it is dark and cold. The woodpile is low.

The next morning, David finds tracks in the snow. There are a group of them going around the house, digging into the meat cache. The rest of the elk is gone. The paw prints are big and confused, mingling with each other. What strikes David, more than the impressions of claws or the number of tracks, what makes him cold, is that there are boot tracks amongst them. He studies the pattern of the tread and thinks it has to be Michael. David is not good at reading tracks—doesn't think Michael is either—and so he has no way of knowing which came first, man or wolf.

He does not know how long Michael has been gone. It snows, the wind blows, days sift over him. David lucks into a rabbit in the draw below the house. His hands tremble as he skins it and he does a bad job. Scrape the flesh and he almost eats it raw.

Imagines tearing into it with his teeth, crunching bone. Instead he cuts it up and brings a pot to boil.

The wind blows harder that night. It tears at the house on its bare promontory. Stupid to build a house here, really. It's at the mercy of the weather, ready to be buffeted into oblivion. The windows shake and David pictures them shattering in the wind, the glass flying fine as dust into the kitchen and winter rushing in. He shivers.

The door knocks in its frame. David looks at it as he edges closer to the fire. Another knock and he realizes that it isn't the wind. His rifle leans against the wall by the door. Stupid. He clutches the knife he used to skin the rabbit and eases toward the gun. Crouches. Keep your shadow off the window over the door. Another knock, but he has the gun in his hand. Tuck knife into belt. Listen.

Another blow to the door and it sounds like an open hand beating at the wood or else a paw, like a dog wanting in. David hesitates. With rifle pointed toward door, he reaches for the knob. He flings the door open and points the rifle. A ragged figure of a man on the ground looks up at him. Matted, mangy hair hangs over his face. Bushy beard a tangled mess.

"Michael," David says.

David pulls Michael into the kitchen because Michael cannot walk. He's shivering and his coat and pants are torn. Michael's boots are caked with mud, but at least they seem intact. David looks down at him shaking on the floor, his teeth chattering, and wonders what to do.

"What happened to you?" he asks as he kneels and starts to unzip Michael's coat. Michael struggles against him at first, but then collapses, exhausted. He allows David to take off his jacket and boots—swollen feet bruised and blistered beneath reeking wool socks. Then David starts water boiling for a bath and brings a glass for Michael to drink in sputtering gulps.

Michael's eyes are red, narrow, and won't meet his. David leads him to the bathtub, thankful he is able to stand and take faltering steps. He strips off Michael's pants, shirt, and long underwear, revealing a thin and bruised body. A long gash on his side. David takes off his own clothes so they won't get wet and brings the bucket of water.

"It'll feel good," he tells Michael, who is curled in the tub and shaking.

Michael jerks when the steaming water falls over him, but he allows David to wash him. Gentle hands massaging soap into scalp, into beard, over his chest, arms, and legs. He has Michael lean forward and pours water over him again, careful to get all the soap behind his ears. The mud and grit wash away. David looks at the cut on Michael's side and wishes he had rubbing alcohol. Something to clean it out more than soap. That much he knows. Keep a wound clean. Instead he finds cotton balls and masking tape. Not great, but better than nothing. Then he dresses Michael in fresh clothes and leads him to the bed where he collapses into immediate sleep.

Michael sleeps the following day and the next. When he wakes, he remains silent, but readily eats the beans David gives him. David wishes he had more, meat of some kind, but he ate all the rabbit and he is afraid to leave Michael in such a weak condition. Besides, outside the wind is laced with snow and it would be foolish to venture out.

Despite his silence, despite his weakness, it is nice to have Michael back in the house again. A conscious presence that is not David. The room feels warmer with another person in it, it feels more secure. David no longer asks him any questions — where is your rifle, how did you get that cut, are there others out there — but he talks to him.

"We'll have cornbread with our beans tonight, Michael. Mix it up," he says. And, "Wish that wind would stop. I'm glad we have a fire." This one-sided conversation full of false positivity is meaningless, but at least the words are addressed to another.

Another windy night and David cannot sleep. He sits at the table and watches Michael. Rise and fall of chest in the candlelight.

He is thinking about putting more wood on the fire—uncut branches he gathered that do not burn well—when he hears a noise outside. Growling. Then a whine and yelp. A howl. The canine sounds come from all around, it seems. Michael jerks awake and starts shaking again. David sits down on the mattress and grabs him in a firm hug.

"It's okay," he says, though he's not sure. The growls and whimpers continue, as if a pack of wolves were fighting each other outside. Something slams into the door and they both jump.

"They're outside," David says. "They can't get in."

They are surrounded by howls and snarling. They can hear claws on the wood, on the walls. The wind is blowing, but they can still hear the animal sounds. David holds Michael and the night goes on and on, never ending. The house will fall down and they will be devoured, the flesh torn from their living bodies.

David wakes and it is morning. The wind is calm and the house quiet. He does not remember falling asleep, does not remember when the noises stopped. David is lying in bed. He reaches out his arm and feels that he is alone. Michael has left. His muddy boots still stand in front of the door. His ragged coat still hangs over a chair.

David rushes outside, pulling on his coat. He sees a confusion of wolf tracks in the snow, and, cut into the snow on top of them, human footprints. David grabs his rifle and follows Michael's trail, the bare feet in a crazy pattern that leads down the hill with the wolves. The tracks are speckled with blood. David imagines the cutting cold of snow and ice on bare flesh. Blood that will turn into black frostbite.

The tracks lead him into the trees, up the wild hills. Deeper snow and David postholes with every step. He uses the rifle as a pole, but is soon exhausted. He had not realized how weak he still is, how much his leg still hurts when exerted. David lets himself fall into the snow. He is desperate for Michael, to not be alone, to continue to live.

David's lungs hurt. He thinks if only he can get Michael

back into the house, Michael will get better. He will go back to the strong, capable man David knows him to be. Whatever has happened to him out here —

The woods are silent. David holds his breath. The cold stillness of this place closes in around him like a weight. He raises his gun against whatever is out there, but there is only silence. He stands and hurries back to the safety of the house.

The wolves return that night. David hears the first howls coming far off, echoing across the moonlit field surrounding the house. He's come to hate that sound. Crescent moon, a hungry mouth. David loads the rifle with fresh rounds, slips a box of bullets into the pocket of his coat. He throws open the door and steps outside its rectangle of light.

As his eyes adjust to the darkness, he sees black shapes cutting through the snow. Groups of them, breaking off to surround the house. He holds the rifle steady, let them get closer. Let them feel the hunt as he has felt hunted. A group of shadows feints in from the right. David wheels and fires. They flee. From the left, another shot in that direction, and that group runs off. Movement from in front, David fires, and hears a sound that is not a yelp, is not a howl.

The wolves back off and he can hear them growling, barking from a darkness he cannot see through. David approaches the shape lying in the snow with gun raised. Whimpering. A human figure, crumpled and writhing. Michael. David bends down to him and Michael snarls, lunges. David feels the clip of teeth on his hand. Backs up.

"Why did you come back? Every time," he says to the creature in front of him, one he can no longer recognize. A miserable, broken figure black in the snow. David remembers Michael breaking the neck of a rabbit caught in a trap, but not killed. He told David it was mercy.

"I'm sorry," David says. He fires the rifle at the black shape and it stops moving.

The wolves howl and get closer. David looks back at the house behind him. Light in the windows and through the open door, but it is not home. It looks far away in the darkness, as far away as the Michael smiling and talking with enthusiasm that he remembers. He is alone. He stands in the darkness and cold alone.

DEREK MONG

GO LITTLE BOOK

Like meteors or shipwrecked treasure,
like fool's gold panned from an icy river —

you only surrendered in glistening shards.
My son, meanwhile, wandered a weedy yard.

I see in you the semblance of an old
face unshaved, one molar capped in cold.

To trace your gaze, line by roguish line,
is rank self-pleasure. You'd leave me blind.

Better that you scatter like vultures blown
free from a feast in the double yellow

and hunch on wires in my neighbor's alley.
You grew fat while I left my family

the scraps of my days, a trail of crumbs.
Fly little bastard — head straight for the sun.

CROWS DON'T SAY

Crows fly straight as the black
hands of a schoolroom clock,
from fencerow to fencerow,
triangulating a field of grain.
They calculate hypotenuse,
shortest flight. No Euclid.
Just the glittering eye, the
parsimonious flap of wings.

Part the feathers on a crow's back
and you'd find no Velcro seam,
no hinges or screws. Plain crow
is what you get, feathers so black
they gleam blue. Yet God knows,
crows keep secrets, the workings
of their brains as melancholy as
a censor's pen redacting prose.

In his youth, the old card player
kept a naked dagger in hip pocket,
tip stuck in a cork. Best way to escape
a bad fight is pull the other man down
on top of you, stab him in the gut,
yell "Help! Help!" so everyone
in the bar comes to your rescue,
and you jump up and run away.

When crows rob a nest, they gild
their getaway with hoarse theatrics.
"Help! Help!" they yell, carrying
a fledgling away in tender embrace,
dodging pecks from parent birds.
"Help! Murder! Murder most foul!"
Whose murder is taking place
the crows of course don't say.

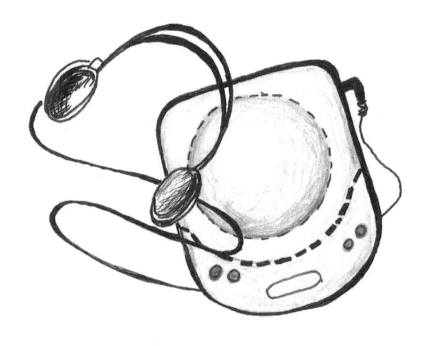

God said to Abraham, 'Kill me a son'
Abe said, 'Man, you must be puttin' me on'

IT'S OUR ALBUM NOW

We were watching a movie that day in eleventh-grade American History. Our teacher, Mr. Etling, who with his white beard and proud posture looked like a shorter Colonel Sanders, rolled out the television cart, dimmed the lights, and hit play on *Newsies*, Disney's 1992 musical based on the 1899 New York City newsboy strike. The film must've correlated with the material we were expected to memorize for the next test, but from the opening number, I struggled to pay attention. I'd recently discovered Bob Dylan's second album of 1965, *Highway 61 Revisited*, and I had a hankering to lose myself in its rock improvisations, its warped images: "The sun's not yellow / It's chicken."

In the back row, I slipped out my CD player, slid on my headphones, and turned the volume on low. Soon the sounds flowing from those black-foam headphones took me over. "Like a Rolling Stone" cast those wool-capped youths behind a gleaming, spitfire soundtrack, causing me to slouch into the sound. Track two, "Tombstone Blues" began,

> The sweet, pretty things are in bed now, of course
> The city fathers, they are trying to endorse
> The reincarnation of Paul Revere's horse . . .

and I pushed up the volume as my body felt alive with tunes relaying American history through a lens of tripped-out skepticism. Shy and quick to blush, I wasn't one to draw attention to myself. But soon Mr. Etling had paused the film and was glaring right at me.

"Mr. Haney," he snapped, as my classmates snickered. He eyed me, and in that moment he must've gathered I wasn't deliberately causing a distraction, but that something wild and compelling within those headphones had pulled me away. "If you're not going to watch the movie," he said in a hard voice tempered with sympathy, "please keep the volume down."

That was all the permission I needed. For the rest of the period I rocked out with my head down, my hands cupped over my ears to shroud and amplify the sound.

While Dylan began to fill the crevices of my brain, my GPA started to sink. The classes were boring, the rules were stupid, and I couldn't wait to get out each day to get stoned with my friends, often before my evening shift at Panera Bread. A few of the readings and writing assignments in senior English managed to hold my attention, though, such as the research paper I wrote on *Highway 61 Revisited*. Inspired for once near the end of my high school career, I compiled a stack of notecards scribbled with insights from books and websites detailing Dylan's thrown-together studio sessions, his associative writing style, his distrust of authority. Fifteen years later, as a graduate student in Boston listening to and writing about every Dylan album in chronological order, I recovered the final draft from my mom's closet on a trip home to Orlando. The pages reveal an ambitious, if convoluted, attempt to understand what my teenage self called "Dylan's first great album."

I don't call it that anymore. Now I say it's Dylan's fourth great album in a row, his second all-time classic (alongside *Freewheelin'*), and arguably his greatest to date, putting it high in the rankings for the greatest album ever. And yes, that same brand of fanboy praise did eventually come through in the essay, along with explanations of Dylan's irregular vocal phrasings and his adamance for extemporaneous takes. Much of the paper, though, is obscured by what I see now as clunky syntax. The first sentence, for example, reads, "In 1965 America there was one number one single released that had enough resentment and anger to join the list of the most important singles of all time." I was talking, of course, about "Like a Rolling Stone," though in inelegant terms—calling it a "number one single" before it was "released," the repetition of the word "one," the attribution of its success to "resentment and anger" alone.

Besides, on the charts, the single only reached number two. The Beatles' "Help!" maintained the top spot.

No matter my shortcomings as a seventeen-year-old stylist, I can take heart that I botched my writing to a far lesser degree than Jonah Lehrer, and with much less at stake. In his third book, 2012's *Imagine: How Creativity Works*, the former science-writing star argued that brilliant strokes of creative genius often occur when an artist has given up trying. Lehrer used as evidence Dylan's '65 tour of England. According to Lehrer, Dylan felt so depleted after the demanding run of shows that he retreated to his cabin outside Woodstock, New York and considered giving up songwriting altogether. "But then," Lehrer wrote, "just when Dylan was most determined to stop creating music, he was overcome with a strange feeling. 'It's a hard thing to describe,' Dylan would later remember. 'It's just this sense that you got something to say.'"

The problem is, Dylan never said that. And thanks to a devout Dylan fanbase glomming onto the artist's every utterance, it didn't take long before someone called Lehrer out. He later admitted to falsifying seven quotes in his book and resigned from his staff job at *The New Yorker*.

In a way, though, the *spirit* of Lehrer's claim about Dylan feeling artistically drained when he wrote "Like a Rolling Stone" at least has *some* relation to the truth. In 2014, the auction house Sotheby's sold a four-page, handwritten manuscript of the near-final lyrics of "Like a Rolling Stone," Dylan's own doodles gracing the margins, for $2 million. According to Sotheby's website, in 1966 Dylan said, "I'd literally quit singing and playing, and I found myself writing this song, this story, this long piece of vomit about twenty pages long."

From those pages, Dylan "boiled down" the writing to four verses, put to music in 3/4 time with a full band in mind. It wasn't until he tried the song in the studio with jazz producer Tom Wilson and a group of hired musicians, including virtuoso guitarist Mike

Bloomfield, that they realized it needed the full complement of 4/4. The first of eleven takes in the new time signature became that number-two single, Dylan's highest chart ranking to date. And it became the subject that saved my grade in senior English.

After high school, I enrolled at Valencia Community College, where I took creative writing, music theory, piano. My freshman year I lived in the duplex Mom had moved us to. She was an elementary school music teacher, and she helped me learn to play songs on the upright piano she bought me for graduation, her long, nimble fingers hovering over mine as I plucked out chords and melodies. At the Orlando public library I delighted to find the *Highway 61 Revisited* sheet music, and I learned "Like a Rolling Stone," "Ballad of a Thin Man," "Desolation Row." The songs provided just the right challenge for my novice abilities. A year later, when a room opened up at my friend Lucas's house, which belonged to rich dad who didn't charge rent, I moved in, leaving the heavy piano behind but bringing the keyboard and drum kit, bongos and harmonicas I'd accrued. The den at Lucas's became our music room, and during house parties I'd hammer out some of my own compositions and some other songs I'd arranged — "Heart of Gold"; Steely Dan's "Peg"; "Signs" by the Five Man Electric Band. For "Like a Rolling Stone," I'd pass around the C harmonica, run through that five-chord song, and incite the guests to howl along: *How does it feeeuhl!*

For the third verse, when Dylan bellows, "You never turned around to see the frowns / On the jugglers and the clowns," I'd instruct the party-goers to *sing with venom!*

Like Dylan, I spat the words encapsulating youth disillusioned. And with each passing year — each falling illusion — "Like a Rolling Stone" gathered more significance. Sometimes I was the "princess" expecting life to be handed to me and becoming gravely disappointed; other times, I was the speaker conveying what he really thought about a clueless peer. At every point, I was more and more on my own. The song just kept becoming more true.

In 2004, *Rolling Stone* ranked the song from which it cribbed its title the number one greatest song of all time. "That must be nice to have as part of your legacy," Ed Bradley remarked in his interview with Dylan that same year.

"Maybe this week," Dylan replied. "But the lists, they change names quite frequently, you know. I don't pay much attention to that." Viewers would be hard-pressed to read much excitement into Dylan's voice as he spoke about authoring the putative greatest song of all time.

Lists. Honors. Awards. None capture the energy of Dylan and his band live in the studio. On the recording, an unlikely organist, Al Kooper, contributes one of the most memorable musical lines in rock & roll, from a high-C vibrating down the major scale. Unlikely because, as Tom Wilson argued while trying to quiet the organ in the mix, "That guy's not an organ player."

"I don't care," said Dylan at the control booth. "Turn the organ up."

Kooper was a young Greenwich Village songwriter invited into the studio just to observe, and maybe play guitar. But when the blues guitarist Michael Bloomfield threw down some licks, Kooper knew he was outclassed. He stashed his guitar and snuck onto the organ where, with his impromptu fills and countermelodies, he earned himself an on-again, off-again spot in Dylan's coterie of musicians and producers for decades to come.

During my listening project, I discovered Kooper now lived in the Greater Boston area, in Somerville. So I sent him an email describing my desire to explore how each Dylan album grew from the last and informed the next, and how the circumstances of Dylan's life could help contextualize the music. It was a longshot, but I thought Kooper might meet me for coffee and riff on these ideas.

To my surprise, he replied within the hour. That he criticized my approach and declined my invitation was less surprising. Because I'd offered praise about his organ playing, he began, "I appreciate your kind remarks," but that acknowledgement shifted swiftly into disapproval: "however I don't agree with the way of thinking you're on in terms of why Bob did this then and thqt now, etc." The typos are his, and I include them here to convey the dashed-off quality of the email; I like to think Kooper was so incensed by my ideas that he couldn't bring himself to read over his reply even once. More likely, he didn't care.

Kooper continued, "A song should be regarded strictly for what it is lyrically, musically and arrangement wise. All the rest is usually conjecture, opinion and folly."

I recognized Kooper's line of thinking from my literature classes in college and grad school. When singer-songwriters were coming up in the mid-twentieth century, New Criticism was the prevailing mode of literary analysis. Practitioners like Cleanth Brooks and John Crowe Ransom promoted works of literature as closed systems, divorced from their creators. W.K. Wimsatt, Jr. and Monroe C. Beardsley articulated this philosophy in their famous text, "The Intentional Fallacy." Their essay argues a reader can't surmise an author's intentions. For that matter, authors themselves can't know what they intended to do on the page. Wimsatt and Beardsley quoted the poet Archibald MacLeish, who wrote during his modernist beginnings, "A poem should not mean / But be." That is, a poem exists for itself, in and of itself.

This notion of autonomy bestows upon a work the status of high art. Christopher Ricks's reading of "The Lonesome Death of Hattie Carroll," for example, in his 2004 book *Dylan's Visions of Sin*, disregards the real event that inspired the song, examining instead how the composition achieves a meaning, tone, and purpose. That purpose, however — shining a light on injustice — remains the guiding principle for the text's arrangement on the page. Ricks's reading only hints at this real-world connection between the lyrics and the events that inspired them. This erasure of author and inspiration has birthed the dubious notion that critics can divorce art from its origins. So it's no wonder Kooper advocated taking a song for "what it is"; he came up in a New-Critical moment which found songwriters struggling for recognition — a recognition fully, finally validated with Dylan's Nobel Prize in Literature. "Music

& poetry should be enjoyed at face value," Kooper concluded, "and if one wishes to study the creator thats another biographical subject altogether."

I understood Kooper as saying that mixing lyrical and musical analysis with biography was irresponsible, and could even devolve into slander. And I was aware of the risks of "conjecture, opinion, and folly" I exposed myself to by exploring Dylan's life alongside his material. But whatever missteps I made would be my own, would reveal something of my subject position, my individuality. I felt the best method was to engage what I brought to the music, and be curious about what Dylan brought, too.

Kooper's conception of art and art criticism was outdated. To be sure, the New Critics made inroads into the line-level functions of meaning and significance within a work of art, especially formal poetry. But as the twentieth century wore on, other critical lenses arose, complicating the role of authorship. Reader-Response theory relied on the reader's perception to project meaning onto a text; Structuralism and Post-Structuralism argued that, as much as anything, the art creates the artist; New-Historicism allowed for a work to take on both a historical and contemporary context. And by the end of the century, a diversification of academia had shed light on how the New Critics' categories of art depended on positions of privilege. The works they preferred adhered to a Eurocentric model of knotty language, formal education, and the leisure time to read, write, and critique. Against these aesthetics, rock & roll fought for the label of art, and Kooper's defensiveness aimed to protect its hard-won prize.

Dylan, for his part, has displayed through the years an awareness of these critical schools. In 2001, at a press conference in Rome promoting his then-latest album, "*Love and Theft*," a reporter asked if he dreaded analysis of his songs. "I don't know," Dylan responded. "A Freudian analysis, you mean? Or German idealism? Or maybe a Freudian Marxist?" The jocularity with which Dylan dished out these terms suggests that these analyses, as esoteric and indecipherable as they are, have little influence on his work. But he's at least familiar with them enough to invoke them offhandedly.

Yet Dylan's work, too, often veils its meaning behind indecipherability; and Dylan has regularly worked to obscure his own message. In 1965, at a press conference in San Francisco, the notoriously well-read Dylan delivered a functional primer to semiotics, or the study of how language relies on symbols and signs. Among the crowd were jovial poets in suits and ties; Dylan perched at the microphone, jittery and simpering. "I think of myself as a song-and-dance man," he said, twice. Nearly a half hour into the event, some of the questioners began to challenge him on not giving genuine answers. "I just know in my own mind that we all have a different idea of all the words we're using," Dylan replied. "Like if I say the word 'house,' we're both going to see a different house, like if I just say the word, right? So, we're using all these other words, like 'mass production' and 'movie magazine,' — we all have a different idea of these words too. So I don't really know what we're saying here."

Except that it *is* possible to know what someone means when they mention a house, or mass production, or movie magazine. A common language relies on agreed upon definitions of those phrases, necessary for people to communicate, for society to function. The difference lies in the various associations each of our minds concoct, all subjective to our own experiences.

In this way, for example, at just the suggestion of *Highway 61's* track three, "It Takes a Lot to Laugh, It Takes a Train to Cry," I hear the opening chords of Dylan's loose barroom piano, his salty-sweet lines about mail trains and the "moon . . . climbing through the trees." I hear the languid harmonica solo at the end giving way to "From a Buick 6," evoking Bloomfield's tight blues riffs that veer away from long, bent notes because in rehearsal Dylan had told him, "I don't want any of that B.B. King stuff." No, following on the heels of Dylan's electric betrayal of the folkniks at the 1965 Newport Folk Festival, he wanted this new material to cook.

At the mention of the title track, "Highway 61 Revisited," I hear that obnoxious slide whistle which Kooper jokingly draped around Dylan's neck in place of his harmonica. I always felt the whistle detracted from the driving rock tune. Then again, I savor how those opening lines, "God said to Abraham, 'Kill me a son' / Abe said, 'Man, you must be puttin' me on'" recount the very origins of Western religion. Simultaneously, Dylan invokes his own musical origins, as the actual Highway 61 runs from Dylan's birthplace of Duluth, Minnesota down through the South, connecting his homeland to the Delta blues.

I hear the songs within the context of my own experience, but I undoubtedly hear the songs.

And even though I'd lost touch with my senior research paper for some fifteen years, I'd retained the residue of that information. How Dylan called the album "vision music," as opposed to some folk record, on the San Francisco radio in December, 1965. How he provided minimal instructions for the band, save for cursory run-throughs of the chord changes and an approving head nod here and there while they vamped and riffed. How Bob Johnston, the Nashville producer who replaced Tom Wilson for every track after "Like a Rolling Stone," took a decidedly hands-off approach. Rather than directing the musicians, he simply canvassed the room with microphones, kept the tapes rolling, and captured everything: the improvised musical conversations, the raw, untutored takes, Dylan's own boisterous wordplay.

I know the album's every sound. With the three songs I learned, I know the feel of the chords beneath my fingers. "You walk into the room with your pencil in your hand," Dylan sings, and I sing, to open "Ballad of a Thin Man." "You see somebody naked and you say, 'Who is that man?'" These lines obscure whether the "You" is Dylan, or the listener, or somebody else. "But something is happening here and you don't know what it is," goes the chorus: "Do you, Mr. Jones?" And now that I've been rebuked by Kooper and gone on to write about Dylan critically—in the close reading sense of the word, but also in the sense of questioning some of his choices—I project myself into this takedown. Now

I'm the music critic who thinks he has a bead on what a song or movement means but almost always misses the mark.

Would Dylan consider me one of those Mr. Joneses he condemned? I pass judgments as I scan this material for meaning—would he approve? Or would he treat me like a member of the press, of whom, Dylan told Bradley, "They're not the judge. God's the judge. The only person you have to think about lying twice to is either yourself and God. The press isn't either of them." Those press members are the ones of whom, in "Ballad of a Thin Man," Dylan sings, "There ought to be a law against your comin' around." His disdain is palpable.

In *Don't Look Back*, D.A. Pennebaker's raucous documentary of Dylan's '65 tour of England, that disdain boils over. Midway through the film, the camera captures an interview between Dylan and a *Time Magazine* reporter. With his sideburns and big, messy curls, his active hands holding a lit cigarette, Dylan rocks back and forth before the much older reporter who, with his slicked-back hair and crooked teeth, maintains a calm expression while he questions the young firebrand. The journalist will attend that night's concert, and Dylan, fed up with all these expectations cast on him by fans and the media alike, admonishes the reporter. "I've got nothing to say about these things I write," Dylan scolds. "I don't write them for any reason. There's no great message." Dylan then proclaims, "I don't need *Time Magazine*. I don't think I'm a folk singer. You'll probably call me a folk singer, but the other people will know better." The reporter's eyes bulge as Dylan says, "I know more about what you do . . . just by looking, you know, than you'll ever know about me. Ever."

If that reporter is Mr. Jones, I don't want to be him. I don't want to catch Dylan's ire for misreading his music. No, I want my idol to like me back. I want to be his friend—but not his best friend, because, in '84, when Kurt Loder asked who his best friend was, Dylan struggled to say. "A best friend is someone who's gonna die for you . . . Yeah, I'd be miserable trying to think who my best friend is." And in 2012, Dylan told Jonathan Lethem the same thing about love: "When someone will die for you, that's love."

I mean, come on—I'm not *Jesus!*

Besides, even if I'd been frequenting the same gatherings as him in mid-'60s Manhattan, I doubt he would've paid me any positive attention. Michael Bloomfield described Dylan's cruel cliquishness in a '75 interview, recalling that Dylan, Grossman, and inner-circle hanger-on Bobby Neuwirth "had this game they would play" consisting of "intense put-downs of almost every human being that existed but the very few people in their aura that they didn't do this to." If Kooper's reaction is any indication, my close reading, my analyzing, my fawning would've subjected me to their venom.

And I see their point, I do: music and poetry work best in those rarified realms; any attempt to rationalize or project them into other cultural arenas bastardizes the material. Only as shining artifacts of pure creation can the songs be understood. These arguments are convincing, but only to a point, because meaning happens anyway, in the audience's minds and hearts. The careful critic strives to make her own art. She wants to be "that man" too, the artist whose creations survive and exert their influence through the ages. All writers want to be "that man."

Except that, being "that man" means relinquishing control. Once music reaches an audience, it belongs to them as much as it does the performer. No one can tell me *Highway 61 Revisited*'s track six, "Queen Jane Approximately," with its loose and jangly sound, doesn't belong to me now. Same with track eight, "Tom Thumb's Blues," whose spirited chords were somehow beyond my skills in junior college but whose jabs—"my doctor won't even say what it is I've got," and "the cops don't need you, and man, they expect the same"—have burrowed into my mind's most rebellious recesses. And the final track, "Desolation Row," allows me to reminisce about how those notes sound from my long-ago re-sold upright piano, even though the eleven-minute track doesn't feature a keyboard instrument. Three musicians play on the track: Dylan, with his guitar and harmonica, Russ Savakus on bass, and a second acoustic played by Nashville ace Charlie McCoy. The resulting performance ensues like an epic fever-dream, vivid and allusive. The guitars speak to each other, cry to each other by the crescendo, their fervid picking and strumming shuttling this album to a close.

Highway 61 Revisited is Dylan's album, but it's my album — our album — too. I learned the songs; I studied the methods and arrangements; I poured myself into that high school senior research paper. It's in my bones. It's what I do, even if Dylan and Kooper would have it otherwise.

AIR-BORN FUGUES

after Whalers *c.1845*

Something inexplicable just occurred.
A leap into an edge of light. Maybe not
what our attention's meant to be
focused on — the whale and the darkness

below it, water tinged with its blood
and the fervor of sharks. Fractures
of light, individual brush strokes,
could be the memory of terns lured

by the whale's air-borne fugue. The violence
of the fluttering sails, death given form.
None of this distracts from the mystery

that glimmers in the thrown-off water
almost out of the picture — the signature
of that which was briefly here and is gone.

FULL OF STRINGS AND FORGIVENESS

after Walker Evans' Westchester, New York, Farmhouse, 1931

Such stillness fractures. The limbs of
a mid-winter tree crack in the glare
of the white this farmhouse was painted,
a Ford's leather seats tell varied stories
of how bodies have moved in the grooves
that form runes only ghosts could hope to
decipher. *Huddled* is a music here,
with lyrics that only sound familiar

from enough of a distance. Even
the landscape hunkers up close. Encroaching,
some say. Others say enveloping. This
farmhouse settles nights under the weight
of ghosts who spent their lives trying to
keep the landscape at bay. Nights the moon
is full, ghosts watch, from attic windows,
the scurrying grace of small animals
and bow to one another and dance

as if they wore tuxes and gowns and graced
some antique ballroom far off in town,
imagining a music full of strings
and forgiveness. The heat being formed
by the memories of the bodies
they used to dance in reminds the ghosts
how they'd hold each other, alive,
the music so alluring they couldn't resist.

THE UNPREDICTABILITY
OF THE PAST

after Walker Evans' New Orleans, 1935

It's been said mystery waits around
the next corner, and light,
with something as simple as motion,
can blur anything into a disguise,
one readily seen past. Lit up
by an unpredictable angle
of sunlight, what looks to be
a lad in knickers out in the dead

middle of a street empty enough
to mimic ruins seems to be after
something not visible, or maybe
he's running from the Marine Bar
where his father was just shot down.
To accept that's a lot. Everything
calm in this moment. Still. Only
the boy's in motion. Blurred. It must be

a game he's caught up in. The severe
early morning angle of sun carves
this corner into clarity. It would have
to be a decision, to not notice
the White Entrance sign and know what is
really going on. Forgive the boy
whatever game he's playing. Forgive
the sun for vision. Forgive the past
for continuing to be what it was.

For tuna, make it salty, and don't
be frugal with the mayonnaise.

ON OCCASION OF YOUR NEW JOB, CONGRATULATIONS AND A RULE OR TWO

Ms. Johns,

I like to think that we might not meet. If you could keep it that way, I'd be grateful. I've enclosed my schedule below, so you can time your own movements around my habits. I hope your bedroom is to your liking; never fear, there are no cameras in there. There are cameras in every other room, however, and a great deal in the kitchen. The ingredients in there are also monitored by calorie scanners — if you produce anything lacking the requisite calories, an alarm will sound and you will be fired, without so much as a severance credit.

There's only one law in here, and that's that I get to eat whatever I want, so long as its health index is below 30%. Below 30% means anything delicious, nothing nutritious. Your job is to do the cooking: You might have noticed that I'm monstrously fat. It's fine, you can say so. I've come to take it as a compliment.

We air every morning at 6 AM, 9 AM and 10.30 AM (for a mid-morning snack). Lunch is prompt at 12.15 and I like to nap on the living room couch until 4. At a quarter after, I eat sandwiches: turkey or tuna will do. If turkey, light on the cheese and heavy on the mustard. For tuna, make it salty, and don't be frugal with the mayonnaise.

Dinner is at 6.30, with a dessert course no later than 7 o'clock, so the kids can watch before bed. At 10PM I eat a final snack, and drink a snifter or two of rum, or gin.

(This list of my dietary requirements can also be found in your welcome pack.)

Help yourself to music and books. Please play nothing on the stereo while the show is airing. I CAREFULLY curate the soundtrack to my meals, and match them to the mood I'm trying to convey. Our show is often the only pleasure our viewers receive, certainly gastronomically speaking. As such, it is ESSENTIAL that our show run smoothly. If you encroach upon a live recording, for any reason beyond the life or death, you will be fired. Again, you will receive no bonus credits.

You may help yourself to any of the Vicarious Chow™ merchandise from the store room below. However, please do not wear any of the identifying apparel outside the house. Understand, that while we are a necessary component of the fabric of society (indeed, the public generally watches me with pleasure in their hearts), they are nonetheless prone to fits of *extremely prejudiced jealousy*. My predecessor was doing very well to live to thirty-four, and with only minor cholesterol issues, before he was cut down on the street while ill-advisedly wearing a *VC* baseball cap. Of course his generally-nutrified glow may have given him away long before the cap was spotted. If you are ever accosted and recognised, my only advice for you is: run. Run, run, as fast as you can. Remember the old nursery rhyme:

> Run, run as fast as you can,
> You can't catch me,
> Because you're fucking starving and I'm generally pretty well fed, all things considered, so you'll probably collapse in a mile or two and vomit up some stomach acid.

I don't know if that's how the rhyme originally went, but it's certainly applicable to our business.

I will not lie to you when I say that the reason your new job was vacant has much to do with the death of your predecessor. Walking with her children (you don't have children, do you? SO irresponsible in this day and age) across Riverside Park, she was stopped by what can only be described as an angry mob. They didn't have actual pitchforks, so far as I know, or flaming torches, but they were certainly *metaphorically* carrying both objects, as well as some *literal* very sharp axes, which they used to dismember both her and her children. As far as I recall they were finding parts of them up and down the Hudson river for weeks afterwards. A child would be digging around in the sandpit and POP there's a toe, or WHOOSH there's a nose, or a part of a shin.

Do not fear unnecessarily, however. The lesson there is that *she did not run.* She tried to explain to them that their only having 10 food-credits a week was part of their moral duty as part of a society riven by despicable overpopulation, which is of course, true. And most sensible people would not argue with her, except it's hard to be sensible when your child is starving and your stomach is hurting and you feel like you are rotting from your inside out, which I hear is what hunger feels like.

At the age of 35, chances are that I will die of a heart attack within the next year or so, at which point my successor, whomsoever the lottery chooses, may keep you employed. On the other hand, he or she may not.

As scary as that all may sound, try to remember that what we are doing is *essentially a good thing.* There is not enough food, that is a simple fact, yet still the little people clamour to be reminded of the joys of overeating. To eat vicariously through me, as it were, is all most of them have. That and a crust or two per day.

Note, I call them the 'little people' in my previous paragraph not because I consider myself more important than them, but only because they're all *extremely* thin.

My final advice to you is the following: Do not eat too much. Though your credits during my employ will be unlimited, they may not always be that way, should you lose your position. Cast onto the street as an overweight woman, chances are the people will eat you. After I die, they will eat me too.

I have come to accept that there is no god, nor a heaven to which my body might travel. If I have a soul, I dearly hope it is fed to the masses, and that it be delicious.

My post-final advice is that whipped cream goes with *absolutely everything*.

Welcome to the Vicarious Chow™ family.

Warm regards,

Tony Jerez,
17th Praegustator of the People, incumbent.

[MASTERS FROM MY SPIRITUAL TRADITION BECAME SO STILL]

Masters from my spiritual tradition became so still they watched existence simmer in a tremendous kettle (their hearts.) They watched it ALL from such great heights, then headed home to simmer pots of jasmine rice. Hungry hospital voices call to me & (gently now) I touch each pain. *O mani padme ohm.* Slip a dollar in the hungry palm of each beggar. Tape guerilla art to brick alleys in Denver. Plant a kiss on the forehead of one who has left us. Said mother, "If we're just going to die in the end, why keep living?" (Brutal & unhinged.) All I could say was, "I'm here for you, so tell me where it hurts." Ask me to show up & I'll show up. Opening my arms into black flowers, purple flowers. *May I be a vessel for the healing.* "On a scale of 1-10," mother said, "I'm nearly dead." "The kingdom of God," Fred Rogers consoles, "is for the brokenhearted."

BIRD BONES

Sadness is only in the body

a bird lays on a frozen field
plain as the surface of a lake

if a single thing in this world moved or if the world
shifted its weight, the body
would let go

the misdirection of the feathers
and pointed grass
would press together like words in a book—forged iron—
staring at each other each hour and knowing
they must always long for closeness

but everything (everything: the moon, a man's arrogance and
     desire, turnips, revolution, mortgage
approvals, lost ships) exists in their distance

And so my body also freezes the way all war
should freeze after a death

Trust is a broken blade of glass
(it cannot be held tightly)
so I unfold the way a lake
first warms in the middle

if I were to touch you
words would spill and rip into one another,
the bird's thin bones would know the weight of the dirt,
the earth's slow jaws, I would digest everything,
everything, the victor,
eating alone.

I hit on everything, even when my hand was too high.

IN CASE OF EMERGENCY

There's nothing like a grocery store before sunrise. I like to go around 4 a.m. on nights when I wake up sweaty and gasping and can't fall back to sleep. At that hour I'm usually the only customer in the store, and the stock boys have finished their shifts, leaving each shelf in perfect order. Every cereal box and can of soup has been pulled forward and perfectly aligned so that everywhere you look is like an Andy Warhol print. It's the only time that it's hard for me to feel down, surrounded by so much brightness and commodification at a time when most people are unconscious.

One morning, in the bakery corner, a row of croissants glowed beneath the thick plastic of the case. I could tell they were still warm without even touching them. It moved me, this sense of order that flowed through the store and crescendoed into something so ancient and miraculous as bread.

I slid two croissants into a brown paper sack and snuck them into the bathroom, abandoning my cart momentarily. Locked inside a stall, I started to devour a roll. It was cold and stale, and I gagged as the first mouthful squeezed down my throat. After a few bites, I didn't have the energy to chew anymore and threw the remains into the trash. Shoplifting is a new preoccupation, but I only take things no one will miss.

At the register, I swiped my debit card and poked YES with the little stylus, then selected $20 cash back. The cashier, a pimply boy with wet-looking hair, handed me the crisp bill wrapped inside the ribbon of the receipt. He called me ma'am.

In the parking lot, I slid the money into an envelope I kept in the back of the glove box, behind napkins and folded maps and the thick, pristine car manual. The little stack of money had grown since I started squirreling away tens and twenties after my weekly shopping trips. I ran my thumb across the bills, savoring the sound like shuffling cards before I put the envelope away and stacked up the paper junk like it was before.

Though Walt never used my car and would never think to look, I wouldn't know what to say if he found it. It wasn't that I couldn't think of a plausible lie—I just didn't know what the truth was myself. I knew that the stash made me feel safe, even optimistic. On rare occasions, I fantasized about leaving. Getting my own studio apartment in a building with squeaky stairs and moldy-smelling carpet. I could rough it out, ask my brother and an old coworker from the bank to help me move a few pieces of furniture, and I would be different . . . It would be like the pilot of a sitcom. But mostly, the envelope felt like a parachute pack on an airplane: soothing though unlikely to ever be used. None of these are things a husband wants to hear from his wife.

On the drive home the smell of saguaro blossoms flooded the car with a sweet, dusty smell like rotting cantaloupe. The light outside had turned blue-gray, revealing just the white flowers that frosted the tops of the enormous cacti along the roadside so it looked like they were floating in the dark. Soon the hills around Tucson would flame up in orange light as the sun cleared the edge of the mountains, and the cacti and the flowers would glow together like a single entity. For a day, anyway. The blooms materialize one night, only to drop off and die the next.

As I pulled into our neighborhood a colony of bats swarmed overhead, stuffed with insects and pollen, on their way back to wherever they slept. There were thousands of them pulsing like black static across the sky. I read this article about echolocation, how for all their screaming, bats are sloppy fliers, bouncing into one another like patrons in a crowded nightclub.

My mood sank as I got closer to the house. I tried to examine the feeling, to grip its thread and fish it out. My stomach felt heavy and my chest fluttered, too light. It was Walt.

I was never sure what sort of disposition he'd be in when he woke. His patience with me had been declining for several weeks. When I lost my job as a loan officer he took only a second to indulge his disappointment. He put his palm to his forehead and shut his eyes when I told him about the layoff. "Jesus, Holly. You've got to be kidding," he said, before squeezing my shoulders and telling me, "You'll find something better. I know it."

But his encouragement started to wane. My severance package shriveled away, and my employment benefits were close to tapped out. The more urgency he felt over the situation, the more stagnant I got. I didn't want to find something better. I was relieved to be let go. I'd spent most workdays window shopping on the internet. Putting items into the cart and taking them out again and making wishlists of products I didn't need or even wish for. Thinking about specs for deluxe camping gear or kitchen appliances was the only thing keeping me in the desk chair most days. When I left, I'd had to remove only a Tupperware container and a few ketchup packets from my cubicle. Already I had forgotten most of my coworkers' names. Now Walt would return home on weekdays to find me sprawled on top of the duvet, blinking at the ceiling fan in its lethargic rotation.

Mostly, though, he did his best to sympathize with these mysterious bouts of paralysis, trying to cheer me up with greasy takeout and funny anecdotes. I told him about the depressive fog that lifted just before we met and how a period of melancholia had caused me to flunk out of college fifteen years ago. He seemed sympathetic. He kissed my fingertips and said, "In sickness and in health."

I left out the part about the extension cord in my dorm closet. That part seemed too weird to tell him. I had kept it in there on a hanger, sandwiched in the back between my jacket and one cocktail dress. When I felt particularly glum, I would thread it over the sturdy fixture that housed the sole fluorescent light in the room and stand on the wooden desk chair, sometimes for an hour at a time, with one end of the orange cord wrapped around my neck. He wouldn't have understood the habit, how it was just a big red button that said: PUSH IN CASE OF EMERGENCY.

It had all started to wear on him. He would come home from work to stacks of filthy dishes and our dog, Bonkers, swatting his empty water dish in frustration. A crowd of ants descended upon a half-eaten bologna sandwich that I'd left on the floor next to Walt's side of the bed. On some days, I would hear him cleaning up from our bedroom, slamming the lid on the washing machine or banging the dishes around recklessly. Even when he was in another room, his resentment was sucked up into the return vents and piped through the A/C. I understood. It wasn't fair.

His alarm wouldn't go off for another twenty minutes, so I eased the front door open to avoid waking him. The crinkling of the grocery bags set me on edge. I tiptoed past the hallway and into the kitchen, but when I lifted one of the bags up to set it on the counter, a jar of pasta sauce sliced through a tear in the plastic, nicked the side of the countertop and exploded all over the floor. I heard Walt roll over and groan.

I was on my knees sopping up the red goop and glass shards when I noticed him standing in the doorway.

"You've been out already," he said.

"Thought I'd get an early start."

I was plucking up the last scattered chunks of glass as he poured coffee.

"Got a lot planned for today?"

I thought it might be some kind of joke, so I ignored it and emptied the glass into the trash bin. Then I tossed last week's rotting produce along with it, before unpacking the rest of the fresh apples and pears. Those too would probably be thrown out next week. I think that to an alien this behavior would be interpreted as a pious offering to a mystery deity. A superstitious act to ensure one's health or control the weather.

"Don't forget Martin and Brianne invited us over tonight," he said from the breakfast nook.

"Oh . . ."

"It would be nice of you to show up. Everyone will be there."

Everyone consisted of the friends he'd made through work and their wives. I could tell from his voice that he probably didn't even want me to go. The thought of the noise and card games and their towheaded children crawling across laps, knocking over drinks, was too much.

I went anyway. Brianne got stoned and led me through the house like a museum docent, pointing out new additions, estate sale bargains.

"I was thinking of putting a set of French doors here," she said. "I don't know what I'd put on the adjacent wall though. It's such a strange size. Like a trapezoid. What could go there? Maybe, like, a gallery wall with family pictures or something . . ." Her enthusiasm for interior decorating was overwhelming.

I held my wine glass at chest level and tried, really tried, to look interested, but it started to break my heart, and then it started to scare me. Their marriage had been injured over and over by Martin's affairs. A couple women on Tinder, a girl he met at a concert. This was coping. Constantly shaping and revamping their physical space gave her the illusion of control. Her little son ran up, whacked her in the leg with a sippy cup, and she didn't flinch. When I first met her, I found Brianne's easygoing nature and the glee with which she played hostess intimidating. An organized, fun woman. Who could compete with that?

When we left that night, stumbling toward the door after too much cheap merlot, she pulled me aside and whispered, "You know, as soon as the kids are in school I'll leave him. I really will. And we'll all be happier for it in the long run."

When we got into the car, Walt turned the key in the ignition and leaned back for a moment with his eyes shut. "Brianne's really great, you know. I wonder sometimes if Martin realizes that," he said before backing out of the driveway.

The next morning, I watched from the window above the kitchen sink while Walt and the dog conducted their daily round of fetch. Bonkers's legs churned like machinery across the backyard, revving up clouds of dust from the patchy grass.

The sun was up. He embraced Bonkers in a huge bear hug, scratching his chest and play-biting his ear. They looked like part of a happy family. That's when it occurred to me that he was probably sleeping with Brianne. In movies, stuff like that is a punch to the gut, but I just thought it was an intriguing testament to the fact that you can never really know anyone.

He slammed the tennis ball off the corner of the patio, and the ball soared high into the air. All three of us were gazing up at it when I noticed my left foot was damp. I looked down to see blood seeping into the weave of the kitchen rug, like ink dispersing in water. I had overlooked a sliver of glass.

Walt was headed out of town on business for the next two days, completing a project for the restoration company he'd started. The work varied. Sometimes it consisted of refinishing antique fixtures or repairing disintegrated marble. They took overused, dirty materials and made them gleam again. This particular job was in Albuquerque and involved restoring an entire bank built in the late 1800s. He and the small crew would refinish elevators, tile floors, and marble columns. Even the old vault. The work could be delicate, and Walt often reminded me that "Architecture is art. No doubt about it."

He was at the door to leave, duffle bag slung over one shoulder.

"You'll be all right while I'm gone?" he said. "Please, Holly, this time don't forget the trash. I need you to make an effort."

He wasn't looking at me. He faced the sunlight, eyes closed, savoring the breeze that pushed through the screen door in soft bursts. Already content with the day. This miraculous ability to be satisfied with anything was the reason I first clung to him. I always knew that this optimism is what led him to marry me. He saw boundless potential in all things. He was like the human embodiment of those "Life is Good" t-shirts. You could be annoyed by the attitude, but only because you wish you had it. He kissed me, not on the lips or on the cheek, but even farther away, near where my ear met my face and hugged me goodbye.

Around noon I headed down to the neighborhood pool. School was in session so there wasn't an abundance of screeching preteens slipping around on the burning cement yet. I knew how self-indulgent it would have looked to Walt: the unemployed housewife lazing around the pool. It was a habit I had started about six weeks prior and was the only thing aside from grocery shopping that could motivate me to leave the house. I kept dreaming about water. About being carried away by a rushing stream in sunlight that didn't make my head hurt. So I started going. It would be enough to get just a little momentum, I'd hoped. Most days, I thought I could pull myself out of this. I would swim laps until my stomach throbbed with a good emptiness that reminded me of being a kid, my legs vibrating with exhaustion. The desk job flab that had accumulated around my abdomen melted away. It had made me feel guilty to have it there as I had no excuse for it. Most women my age that I knew had kids, and the soft, crêpey skin around the belly button was something earned.

There, I often ran into Tom, a father from the newest block of the subdivision who ran a web design business out of his basement. I was stretched out absorbing the afternoon heat when he came up, dragging a metal chaise that screeched across the concrete.

"By gosh, by golly. Look, it's Holly," he said. "I'm glad to see you here." He started talking about a local scandal. Some politician who had embezzled public funds and used it on prostitutes. At least that's what I gathered. He talked about it as though I already knew. I was embarrassed to be out of the loop and feigned my way through the conversation like it was a test I had forgotten to study for.

"Caught with his pants down. He's ruined. Don't you think?"

"Absolutely," I said. "Hard to come back from that."

He laughed as he did at everything I said, which made me feel momentarily charismatic. Then he kept going on, about elections, about the future. One-sided conversations like that put me at ease.

He got up to walk to the locker room, and I felt abandoned for some reason. Walt was speeding away from Tucson, getting farther and farther east every second. I followed Tom through the doorway of the tiny building that contained the men's and women's locker rooms. I caught up to him and touched his elbow.

"Hey, Tom. You should come over for dinner tonight."

I thought he looked confused, but it was so dark under the awning compared to the poolside. Like when the lights go out and you keep blinking but still can't see a thing. His face was shadowed, and I couldn't focus, couldn't tell quite how far away it was.

"Walt is out of town," I said, and touched his chest. I let my hand slide down to his belly, and he sighed, peeled it off and cradled it loosely. Bending low, he put his face close to mine so I could see his eyes, his giant pupils fixed on me. My hair was dripping wet down my back and making me shiver.

"Jesus, Holly. Come on. We're both married. What are you *doing*?" He let go of my hand, and it hovered in the air between us. Then he turned and went into the locker room.

When I got home, I crammed some clothes into an old suitcase and left my wedding band on the soap dish. I usually put it there while showering, but this was different, so I held it in my fist for a minute before setting it down.

I hadn't thought about the dog. Really, I wasn't thinking about anything. A lot of the time I feel as though I'm just a body. I close my eyes and try to picture a control panel or a helm at the front of my skull, but when I imagine looking in through the glass there's just an empty captain's chair. Like the person manning the controls has abandoned ship. I couldn't leave him there alone so I loaded up the suitcase and Bonkers into the backseat and hit the highway as fast as I could. Not even ten minutes on 68 West, and the dog whimpered and flopped himself gracelessly over into the passenger seat.

The desire for movement wasn't just irresistible, it was as though my brain and body were gasping for it, and it would kill me to remain stationary. I've heard that some birds have magnetite in their brains that interacts with the earth's magnetic field like a compass, driving them to migrate. I wondered what parts of me that seemed indivisible from my identity could simply be removed with a precise cut of a scalpel.

I kept picturing the coast. I wanted to wade out into the Pacific and disappear. To be buoyed far out to sea and then to sink down and stick to the black floor of the ocean like a starfish.

Bonkers started to get carsick after a few hours. He sat rigid with his head bowed, afraid to look out the window at all the cars whooshing past, and panted anxiously. I wondered if he assumed that Walt and I, as his providers of food, shelter, and entertainment, were responsible for everything he experienced and therefore thought I was the source of his nausea. I felt guilty. A veterinarian I met at a party once told me that dogs express different moods through panting and that some animal shelters play contented panting over speakers to help relax the dogs that are frightened. I remembered this and tried to pant in a way I thought might calm him down, smiling with my tongue out and patting his head as we were passing the Colorado River into Nevada. When I looked back at the road, a monarch butterfly hovered in front of the car for an instant before smashing against the windshield in a horrific burst of orange. I stopped in the middle of the bridge and pressed my forehead into the steering wheel until I got up the courage to turn on the wipers. I ran them for at least ten minutes, people honking and swerving around me, before I could bring myself to look up.

There was no trace of the butterfly. Straight south on the Nevada side of the water was Laughlin. Its small clump of casinos and palm trees stood out in the expanse of flat desert, luring me in like a tacky mirage. I pulled off the highway to rent a room in a riverboat casino. By then it was dusk, and the red boat was lit up, even the paddlebox and smokestacks were speckled with white lights. I grabbed the envelope from the glove box.

After I checked in and paid the steep deposit that was mandatory for cash customers, I snuck Bonkers in past the concierge. It wasn't too difficult with the hordes of people moving through. Worried that he might gnaw on the unfamiliar furniture or rip apart the hideous floral bedspread if left alone, I shut him in the bathroom. The room was off one of the covered decks of the boat that overlooked the Colorado River, and white lattice arches and pillars were lined up all the way down.

Downstairs, on the casino floor, I wandered around through the slot machines and the fog of cigarette smoke. It was impossible to be stuck inside my head in a place like that, with so many people and bright colors. And the noise. All that electronic dinging is crafted to release dopamine whether you are winning or losing. The whole place was red with plush, gold-accented carpet that stretched out like a prairie. The median demographic seemed to be even older than that of your average casino, and neon flashes were sporadically reflected off the glasses of elderly women scattered about. Some had oxygen tanks beside them and wore slippers.

I traded the rest of my cash in for a neat stack of chips. Posted up at a blackjack table, I hit on everything, even when my hand was too high. The dealer would smirk and shake his head, but I kept winning.

"You're on a hot streak, but, sorry to say, you're an idiot," the man next to me said.

"Maybe I just know what I'm doing."

He was a little younger than me, maybe thirty, his height and thinness both jarring, but rather than taunting me, he was smiling with his whole body turned, expecting a conversation.

"It looks that way now," he said, "but you're bound to lose eventually." A dark cocktail was melting on a napkin next to him, the straw chewed to smithereens.

"We all lose eventually, but that doesn't stop anyone from playing."

"You have a boyfriend or something?"

"A husband."

"He here?"

"Not tonight."

"What about kids?"

I shook my head. Even the idea made me wince. I used to think it would be nice. Like that might save me, give me something to think about all day; I knew many people who seemed rejuvenated and obsessed by parenthood. But then I always envisioned driving away with a forgotten infant flying off the roof of the car. And they make cages with their neediness. I knew parenthood would be a trap, a black hole. I often wondered if that was the way Walt felt about me.

"Do you have any?" I asked.

"Yes. Izzy is seven. I know how corny it sounds, but she's the best thing to ever happen to me." He pulled out his phone without my asking and showed a photo of a pretty child with a bad haircut. Then he went into a monologue about custody rights, about how he'd been screwed over by his ex-girlfriend, until I couldn't stand it anymore.

"What are you doing here tonight?" I asked.

He shrugged and almost knocked over a waitress's tray of drinks. "Just this. Trying to win. Child support isn't cheap, you know."

"Let's get out of here," I said.

"Lady, are you crazy? Don't quit now. That must be seven or eight thousand you've got in front of you." I hadn't noticed it was that much. He was louder and drunker than he was a few minutes prior.

"It's just plastic. Come on," I said. I scooped the chips into my handbag and led him off the casino floor, up the stairs to the deck.

In the room, I unbuttoned his shirt and kissed him hard. Our teeth scraped together, and he shoved me onto the comforter.

His hands were alternately too gentle and then too rough. The anticipation I had felt dissolved so fast it was like the needle getting swept off a spinning record.

Afterward, he got up and stumbled toward the bathroom, and before I could warn him the dog was in there, he opened the door. Bonkers snapped out two angry barks before rushing forward and plunging his teeth into the guy's calf. I yanked his collar, holding him back while the guy bounced around the room naked, yelling, "God damn it," over and over. I pulled the dog back into the prison of the bathroom and shut the door behind us. He dug furiously at the space under the door before he let out a mournful howl and jumped into the bathtub. I got in and crouched down next to him, shushing and scratching his neck. The image of the man hopping around, lanky and pale like a cigarette, was fixed in my head, and I couldn't stop laughing. I sat in the tub giggling with tears in my eyes while Bonkers licked my hand.

"What is wrong with you?" the guy yelled. I heard the front door slam and could feel he had left.

After a while I went out onto the deck and gripped the railing, wishing the casino would unmoor itself and float down the river. Then I peered over the edge and saw the concrete foundation coming up out of the water and understood it wasn't even a real boat at all. Walt would have teased me for thinking so.

I went inside to call him, and when I reached inside my handbag to get my cellphone I realized the man had taken all the chips.

"I miss you," Walt said. "Did your day go all right?" He sounded tired.

"Same as ever. Nothing helps. What am I going to do?"

I thought I could hear him roll his eyes.

"You just have to try. Things will get better if you want them to. You have to trust in that."

"No they won't, Walt. You don't get it."

He was so far away, with hundreds of miles of desert and an

entire state between us. His voice felt like a particularly strong transmission coming in from the other side of the galaxy. We were quiet for a minute. It might have been my imagination, but I thought I heard a faint voice somewhere behind the phone on his end.

"I'm doing my best here," he said. "I don't think I can carry you around forever though."

"I know, but I'm trying. You can't say I'm not."

"It sure doesn't feel like it."

After we hung up, I wished I had told him I was sorry. Not about the money or the man who had left my room an hour before, but for expecting him to be a life raft while I was an anchor.

I remember when I was kid, maybe ten or eleven, I was on a school field trip at an art museum. I don't know why I remember it, but I saw this couple holding hands and swinging their arms back and forth, looking like newlyweds. They were standing in front of this gigantic abstract canvas, just shades of green, when the man bent down and tied the woman's shoe, and she kissed the top of his head. When I saw that, I wanted so badly to be older. For the future to just hurry up and get here. I didn't know it would feel like this. I stretched out across the disheveled bed, and when my hand slipped under a pillow, it brushed against a small piece of plastic. It was a fifty-dollar chip. Enough for a tank of gas to get me home or even as far up the California coast as Monterey Bay, if I were lucky. I had all night to decide, but no place was calling to me.

MARIE-ANDRÉE AUCLAIR

WHO WILL TEND TO THE LARES?

She wanted to be
Ulysses returning from his journey
brimming with colourful customs
she never dreamt existed
amazed at the familiar
scents that would greet her back.

But Penelope was the one left to wait
for dawn to dispel distressing longings
for her lover to return
and the hospitals to keep saying
no, we have had no admissions under that name.

Ulysses came back, his stories
spilling out of celebratory wine cups
Penelope, morphed into a Lares goddess
cooked bland food he called comforting
as if home had become bland for him
who refused flamboyant dishes, indifferent
to the temperamental orchids tucked in her hair.

She learned the names of winds, called to them
from the edges of cliffs. But they never replied.

She learned to run and row, sail and fish
all manners of skills, to be ready
when she'd meet her Lorelei, lustily
crash that ship, follow the lure
and dance drunk on Rhine wine.

Would someone, him perhaps
feed their little penates
propitiate the gods for her return?
She would not worry at all
if he had to weave that endless cloth.

PALACE GATE

Mehrangarh Fort, Jodhpur, Rajasthan

[Beside the innermost gate of the fort, carved hand-prints memorialize
women immolated on the funeral pyre of one of the maharajas.]

The hand-prints of the sixteen *satis* are carved in the wall,
colored with red powder (because they were wives), and gold

(for the fire). No, that's not true, red for auspiciousness and
gold for royalty. Red and gold for the colors brides wear. Red the

meat flung off the parapets in the golden dusk to feed the
huge circling kites, to prevent misfortune. Red a ring I stole

from a gift shop in high school. I still wear the ring, and
on my other hand, one band in plain gold, another with three

red rubies. Gold the field of daffodils where my mother
and sister and I were chased out by barking dogs,

red their collars. We thought it would be all right to pick them.
Red the Toyota hatchback that broke after so many years. Gold

the sedan that somebody gave us, that smelled always like
grandparents. Red my blood on the train platform, gold the dirt

on my knees, on my bleeding palms. Red the telephone, but
the shopkeeper had no phonebook. I wept on the counter; a gold

Ganesha looked on from his corner shrine. Red the sandstone palace,
even under whitewash. I never stole anything else.

I pick up the largest rock I think I can heave into the water. This will be a big joke between us.

SHORE STRANGER

My first day in Bar Harbor, Maine, I wandered the woods of Acadia National Park without a map until I found a beach. I sat in the sand as the sun burned my bare back, wet with sweat and from swimming in the cold ocean. A man carried water in a sandcastle bucket to a toddler in a two-piece and a woman wearing a Red Sox hat. Three teenage boys raced barefoot along the edge of the water. Looking east over the Atlantic Ocean, I wondered about what I might learn this week, whom I might meet, and why the blue of the horizon was so much darker than the nearly white blue directly above me.

My second day in Bar Harbor I walked over a sandbar to Bar Island. I left the marked trail to walk through a meadow. The grasses brushing my legs reminded me of a walk near Deep Creek Lake in western Maryland and a woman I used to love.

My third day, I heard a roaring sound across Acadia's Jordan Pond. After walking around the pond, I found a man with the didgeridoo making the noise. He stopped playing to show the long wooden tube to a little girl and boy. I peeked inside myself.

And on this fourth day, I look inside a plastic cup half-buried in leaves beside the path I'm following to the coastline. The browning maple pod in the cup reminds me of when I learned to make a whistling sound with a blade of grass.

Three years before Bar Harbor, my girlfriend and I each sat cross-legged in a grove of trees next to a baseball field, abandoned on this humid, ninety-degree day. My bike, helmet, and backpack lay to the side. Clare, sweating through her polo shirt, leaned forward onto her knees and picked a single blade from the grass between us. She laid it along the inward side of her left thumb and pressed her right thumb symmetrically on top. The knuckles and bases of her thumbs left a narrow, oval gap, like the eye of a Halloween cat. When Clare blew through this gap with pursed lips, the vibration of the grass elicited a high-pitched wail. I told her I had never learned how to make that sound.

"Really?"

I never learned because growing up I never asked for help or experimented with any blades of grass. I didn't like admitting I didn't know how to do things, especially those things I felt I was already supposed to know, the things everyone else knew. In childhood I enjoyed various activities — baseball, altar serving, setting the table — activities that came with rules, standards of perfection, and adults as instructors. What gave me the most difficulty were those simple pastimes with no method of learning apart from curiosity and other kids. I never learned how to blow a bubble with bubble gum, how to make a fart sound by sticking my hand in my armpit, how to make a popping sound with my finger in my cheek, how to collect water in my hands and squirt it back out, how to do a cartwheel, how to arch one eyebrow, how to flare my nostrils or wiggle my ears or wink my left eye. I eventually got my right eye to wink. At a summer movie festival a friend in high school taught me how to snap my fingers.

When I remember one moment with Clare, all the others play in my mind: Clare slicing watermelon at a barbecue for my twenty-fourth birthday, Clare dressing slaughtered chickens at a friend's farm, Clare practicing piano — Galuppi, Prokofiev, Debussy, Schumann. Clare in a Facebook photograph with her fiancé on her engagement day, Clare married by now, maybe a mother by now.

The evening I gave Clare a small scented soap, I played baseball with her and her younger brothers. The three boys seemed to like how well I pitched batting practice for them. During cocktail parties at Clare's parents' house, I preferred the company of these boys to that of the adults. I had a lot of growing up to do, and these adults were very grown up. I didn't seem to know the party rules—how to engage others in the right conversations, how to answer when asked how I was. No one offered any instructions. As Clare said the day she ended things with me, her older brothers, parents, and their friends were sarcastic and witty, always teasing and poking fun at one another. I just didn't fit in.

I stand on the rocky shore in Maine holding a smooth circular stone in my hand. The stone is small, not unlike the pebbles that protect the roofs of office buildings from damage. These rooftop stones distribute the body weight of people whose footsteps would otherwise burst the air and water bubbles that form within tar surfaces, cracking the roof. One weekday afternoon two years before Maine, I leaned against the rooftop railing of the building where I worked. Next to me leaned a young woman from another company. We were two attracted strangers who met on the elevator and started skipping work together. On the roof our conversation slowed and I wasn't sure if I was ready to kiss her. Instead I picked up a stone and hurled it onto the roof of the adjacent building.

The stone I'm holding in Maine also resembles the pebbles that make up the path across the top of a dam in Pennsylvania that I'd visited the prior winter with several friends and their children. The boys were throwing stones off the dam. I also wanted to see how far I could toss one. As a stone left my hand, I heard one father yell out his children's names—"Matteo! Gabriele!"

A moment ago I skipped one stone on Maine's Mt. Desert Narrows and frowned when it plopped in the water after bouncing just once. As a child I'd been too impatient to learn to skip well. Even still, I hope my next stone will jump four, five, or six times.

I want this stone to skip for the old stranger standing to my right. Minutes earlier I had watched from a distance down the shore as this man in a purple button-down shirt tucked into black slacks picked up, inspected, and dropped stones. The clack of each drop interrupted the softly lapping water of low tide. I approached the man with the thought that he must be a geologist or biologist, able to teach me something. As I came close, he nodded at me and bent down for another stone. I asked him whether he had found anything interesting. Without answering, he stood up and faced me.

"Find anything interesting?" I repeated. That very morning I had asked the same question to a man off the trail on Cadillac Mountain in Acadia. He gave me fresh blueberries to eat with him. And two days earlier, I had asked the question to a man investigating trees off the trail on Bar Island. I learned that male deer leave slashes in the bark of tree trunks from rubbing the velvet off their antlers to mark their presence.

Not every encounter goes as I hope, even with friends. Sometimes I guess wrong about body language and shared moments. Before another hike I'd dropped my plastic water bottle. Its impact with the gravel parking lot made a small hole on the bottom. I found that I could squirt a stream of water by squeezing the bottle. Just for fun and oblivious to the expensive coat from Milan she sported, I squirted one friend. She asked me when I was finally going to grow up and stop acting like a child. It was about time.

That hike with my well-dressed friend ended at a small waterfall. Another friend's son dropped a plastic gun into a pool at the base of the cascade. Reaching too far for the gun, I slipped partway into the water. With my legs submerged, I dunked my head into the pool, keeping my eyes open so I could find the toy. Moments later, I wrung out my shirt and pants behind some trees, my bare feet standing on soaked shoes, the knees of my pale legs buckling. When we walked back to the cars, I held a little girl's hand, squeezing and shivering and using my arm to part overgrowth blocking the trail.

"Find anything interesting?"

Standing on the shoreline rocks, the old man's facial expression—raised eyebrows, open mouth, shaking head— conveyed that he didn't speak English. I pointed to the four stones the man held in his hand, two smooth and gray, two jagged with white streaks. The man dropped one on the ground. It smashed against the rocks.

"Clang," the man seemed to say. At least that's what the word sounded like. I repeated it, unsure of myself: "Clang?"

The man said the word again as he dropped another stone. He handed his two remaining stones to me. I dropped them. The man gave me a toothy, yellow smile with a right incisor that jutted forward.

I picked up a stone but, instead of dropping it, threw it against a large rock nearby. It ricocheted several feet away from us. We both gasped approval. I picked up another stone and threw it even harder against the same rock. Again it ricocheted away. The man picked up a larger stone for himself. Instead of rearing back to hurl it, he reached his arms out in front and let go. It banged against the rocks at our feet.

Growing up, my favorite game was "catch, not miss." My father and I had a recurring goal before dinner of one hundred tosses without dropping a ball. A baseball makes a thwacking sound like a cracking whip when caught in the pocket of a glove. A ball caught on the palm might pop out of the glove as the hand squeezes it, plopping onto the ground. As we neared one hundred, I often became hesitant. I stopped trusting muscle memory. I no longer followed through, such that after releasing the ball my right hand continued in motion and ended up by my left waist. Instead I held up, freezing my arm in front of me as if placing the ball in "the glove that never missed," our name for my father's mitt. "Don't aim, just throw it," he tried to coach.

Every dinner my three brothers and I repeated our own particular mistakes. William, the first, opened his mouth too wide. Joseph, the second, the other middle child, was too picky. James, the fourth, a lefty, twisted his wrist too much when he held silverware. I struggled verbally. The sibilant S. I learned to avoid the pronoun *she* and the verb *see*. Sometimes my father caught on and made me attempt the avoided word. We repeated

147

for one another, over and over, the same simple tongue twister. The rest of the family ate in silence, opening their mouths wide, refusing their greens, twisting their wrists. "Sally sells seashells by the seashore." "Sally sells seashells by the seashore."

My father used to tell stories at dinner. Once when he was ten years old and walking from school to the boarding house where his family lived for a time, the landlady told him to come listen to the radio with her on the porch. On that day in the middle of the afternoon Bill Mazeroski hit a walk-off home run for the Pittsburgh Pirates in the seventh game of the World Series against the New York Yankees. Listening on the radio to the greatest game ever played hooked him on baseball for life. Another time, his father took him to Griffith Stadium, the old home of the Washington Senators. In that game Mickey Mantle for the Yankees hit a home run that struck one of the light poles.

In the backyard I imagined hitting winning home runs and trotted around our bases, patches of dirt where the grass had died from repeated trampling. I also practiced more seriously, throwing baseballs against an old log. One Christmas my parents bought me what I called a "bounce-backer," a metal frame laced with string webbing against which a baseball could be thrown for pitching and fielding practice. I played with the bounce-backer every day. On snow days I trudged through the accumulation to throw a ball against the webbing and watched the snowflakes fall. On sunny days I imagined myself playing different positions, especially third base, like Cal Ripken Jr. of the Baltimore Orioles. If I didn't play a perfect game—fielding twenty-seven straight grounders and making twenty-seven good throws—I lost.

During one baseball practice in the third grade, my teammates and I struggled to catch the high fly balls our coach hit for us. Afterward I told my father, "Mr. Jones said it's good enough if we get our glove on the ball, even if we don't catch it." My father grunted. I felt proud of him and embarrassed by my comment. My freshman year in high school, I struck out the few times I got to bat off the bench. "Three good hacks, Andrew," my father told me one time in the car. "You can't step in the box and say you're going to hit a single or a double, but you can go up there and tell yourself you're looking for three good ones and you'll take three good hacks."

I hurled a stone into the Maine waters. The man didn't react to the splash but held up a smaller, smooth stone to me. He tried to skip it. He threw overhand, only with his knees bent low. The stone bounced once and fell into the water. I tried for myself, with a similar result. The man searched around before selecting his next stone. He dragged his finger around the edge, indicating for me that it was round. He laid his finger across the width of the stone, feeling for me that it was smooth. He skipped it. Two bounces.

Now I try again, smooth circular stone in hand, wanting it to skip well to extend this moment with the man. I lean down slightly to my right and release it with a sidearm twist, like a submarine baseball pitcher. Satisfied when I see it bounce four times, I turn to the man. He smiles again, with the jutting incisor, but I wonder if I'm testing his patience. I don't want to spoil this moment by staying too long. I pick up the largest rock I think I can heave into the water. This will be a big joke between us. When I turn the large rock over, I see three snails with black shells. I show them to the man, who picks one off and flips it over. The animal sucks itself back into its shell. The man holds the snail in front of me and makes a scooping motion with his other hand, which he continues up to his mouth. Still holding the large rock, I stick my tongue out and lean in until it's just a few centimeters from the snail. He chuckles and places it back on the rock.

The man walks to the water, squats, and washes his hands. I follow and do the same. I see more snails in the water and point at them. Again the man makes a scooping motion. I nod, trying to convey that I understand that snails can be eaten. Maybe the man means something else.

Standing up, he says to me, "I don't speak English." He says it haltingly, as if he knows only this one phrase. I reply speaking quickly that I figured as much, and I ask where he's from, but the man doesn't seem to understand me. I point at myself, then stick out my right hand and say my name. Taking my hand, he says his own. Then he says, "Beijing." I say, "Washington." He nods and returns to dropping rocks.

Further down the shore I see a young boy digging amid the rocks. The boy calls out to his father, seated on a chair in the shade with a smartphone in his hands.

"If I find any crabs, come and look."

The father says he will.

As I watch the boy dig for crabs, the buoys of lobster traps bob offshore. In the distance a few final walkers cross the sandbar from the island back to the harbor. The tide is coming in. Crushing seaweed with my toes and looking at the water, I open my eyes wide to see the blues—the blue of each ripple breaking on the surface, the dark blues of deep water, the light blues of sunny patches, the blues and whites of the sky.

Two years before Maine, on a boardwalk in Bethany Beach, Delaware, I had asked a friend—a priest, painter, muralist, and author—what he was thinking about. "Oh, not really thinking about anything, just looking at all the colors out there," he answered.

From the Bethany boardwalk I looked out at the ocean. Boats trawled sand to rebuild the eroding beach and white birds skimmed the surface of the water. "I'm sorry to say this, but what do you mean, 'all the colors'?"

My father came to this same strip of Bethany sand on vacation when he was a child, after his family moved cross-country from Colorado to Maryland—five children, one grandma, one dog in a station wagon before air conditioning. One story goes that Rex barked out the window at some buffalo grazing in South Dakota. They came after the moving car and got the bumper. My family vacationed in Delaware like his family had, where his family had—a neighborhood of beach houses surrounded by tall pine trees. Sometimes we found turtles plodding among the needles.

My father taught me to swim in the same ocean where he'd learned forty years earlier. We let small waves pick us off our feet. We dove into larger ones. We coasted with smooth ones back into shore. As I got older, I started to push out past the breaking water and float on my back, my feet dangling below the surface. I liked to sink deep. I liked to push down with outstretched arms to where the water gets blacker, even to eyes already closed, to where the water gets colder around the ankles, the stomach, the cheeks.

When I tired, I joined my brothers on shore. We built mounds of sand that we protected from the ocean with walls and moats and our bodies. With time the waves leveled the mounds and broadened the moats into puddles. I sat in the puddles with my older brother, Joseph, the other middle child of the family. He has Down syndrome. We scooped our hands deep into the wet sand, spreading our fingers through the muck. Large waves pushed us around, filling our pockets with sand and giving us wedgies with the suits' inner lining. We drilled our hands down deeper, spitting the saltwater that splashed into our mouths.

After we found sand crabs, we showed them to our parents in their beach chairs at the top of the surf, a few feet away. One of Joseph's interests, aside from catching sand crabs, is birth order. He's the second son. I'm the third. I stood before my parents' beach chairs at the top of the surf, the waves just reaching my ankles, my back wet with sweat and saltwater, a sand crab squiggling in my palm, the third son of a third son.

THE DISPOSITION OF OPEN SPACES

Was it my own behavior that brought me here, to this city, this park, this bench, to these halcyon hours of pickles, sodas, and chips with children running euphorically among the picnic blankets and beautiful hot rods crawling down the service roads? Perhaps it is only a side-effect of American social mobility in stasis. Still, in a silent hour of childhood, my BMX bike stands on the slowly draining lawn under late summer, late evening sunlight. I have been repeatedly moved by geology. Also, seasonal disorders. These last degenerating days of summer; other early autumns. Tangible, temperamental, a little threatening, saturated, and daft. Such daily banalities inflect a broad benevolence, reading books and fingering chords, toweling dishes and sorting foods, waiting for personality to suddenly soar. In the meantime, I'm torqued by the tangent much more than the properly settling point. Love is not only lived, but a concept felt to define a panoply of complex emotions that can't be called false. There may be a feeling that joy has been stolen or otherwise lost; do not worry, it is only the texture of the urban form in August, nothing more. The late warmth of these earliest days may reveal themselves to have been a tether for truer departures to come. You will dream, or have dreamed, of a foreground that is deeply recessed. All at once, you feel the slight pressure of another's hand in yours. A long ways past, a good ways gone. In the moments of greatest immersion, it is right to drift back to sleep. The afternoon has grown too specific to shake. But all that pleased my love was pleasing, you say. Hey. Wake up. Get walking. It's washing day.

STITCHES

Each day at the Y she's there
before me, already immersed,

and when I climb from the pool
she's still swimming —

white braid bisecting her back,
long scar vanishing

down the front of her red suit.
She might be sixty, sixty-five, seventy,

her shoulders made broad
by endless breastrokes.

Her arms glint,
pierce the aquamarine silk,

as she stitches and restitches her lane,
like a seam she's afraid

might unravel. She reaches the wall,
pushes off hard, doubles back

refuses to rest against the forces
that wear a garment thin,

tear it in half.

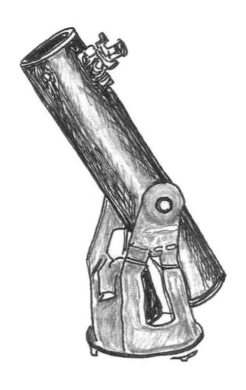

"Mia," he said. His breath smelled like her
grandfather's pipe. "Find Capella."

REFRAINS

1. Poetry

Horacio thought Dr. Palmer's poetry sucked. She wrote about skeletons and flowers and light and dumb insects. He didn't understand any of it. But he loved to watch her legs, extending from a short summer skirt, flex magnificently as she underlined words on the chalkboard: *anapest, allegory, alliteration.*

She appeared on the jacket of her slim volume of poetry, required reading for the class, in a bowtie and horn-rimmed glasses, as if in disguise. Now, a decade after its publication, her hair was an unnatural shade of red. She wore too much makeup. Her eyes were strange; they appeared to change color according to her mood. But Horacio approved of her legs.

He didn't gossip about her the way the others did, whispering over student union tacos. He felt embarrassed for her when she recited her poems aloud in a voice at once proud and self-conscious. He wondered where she spent her nights. Did she rent a studio apartment near the university? Did she cook, or order takeout? Did she step out of her little skirts the moment she walked through the door? He thought she probably did, and then she probably tucked her dead-end hair into a ponytail, pulled on a pair of boxer shorts that had belonged to one of her ex-boyfriends, and ordered a meat-lover's pizza. He smiled to himself as he imagined her taking a big bite.

Tonight she read a poem about a honeybee inseminating a sunflower. Horacio half-listened until the cellphone in his front pocket vibrated. He extracted it to discover a text message from Mia: *going to library after lab xo.* He ran his thumb tenderly over the letters.

Dr. Palmer called on him. He had not heard the question. "I don't know," he answered, contemplating her long legs. She pursed her lips and gave a deep sigh of resignation, as if accustomed to disappointment. Every day she seemed tired.

"Pay attention, Horacio," she said.

"Yes, ma'am," he replied, with only a hint of sarcasm.

2. *Astronomy*

Across campus, Horacio's girlfriend Mia stood apart from her classmates atop the physics building. It was a balmy spring night, late in the semester, and she had begun to sweat. The crop of cannon-shaped telescopes mounted to the roof unnerved her. She could not afford to fail.

The lab assistant was a wannabe hipster with a patchy beard and a side-part. He constantly licked his lips and bragged about how he had made the dean's list every semester during his undergraduate *career*. His skinny jeans were no-name and his zip-front sweaters all had holes in the elbows. But he gave the exams, and rumor had it he was susceptible to certain unspecified charms. Mia gripped her flashlight as he led her by the arm to one of the telescopes, where he expected her to demonstrate what she had supposedly learned.

"Mia," he said. His breath smelled like her grandfather's pipe. "Find Capella."

"Aren't you hot?" She aimed her flashlight at his mustard-yellow sweater.

"Capella," he said. "Find it. Now."

She tucked the flashlight into her backpack, cleared her throat and wiped her hands on her leggings. She adjusted her ponytail, shifted her weight from one foot to the other and fiddled with the telescope's focus knob. Then she surrendered. "I don't know where it is."

"You don't know where it is," he said. "Capella."

"Capella." She shrugged and watched his tongue dart across

his upper lip.

"How about Procyon?" Mia shook her head. She hated herself for having thought the class would be an easy way to satisfy her science requirement.

"Well," the lab assistant said, patting her once on the shoulder. He pulled a small notebook and a stubby pencil from the back pocket of his skinny jeans.

Mia smiled desperately. She would lose her scholarship. If only she were prettier. In high school they had called her *Mia Mouse.* "Do you take bribes?" She tried to make it sound like a joke.

The lab assistant shut his notebook, sighed and gazed up into the starry night sky.

"Cash?" Mia said. She thought about Horacio, sitting in his stupid poetry class. A stab of shame hit her stomach. She would never tell him about this.

The lab assistant's laugh sounded like a wheeze. "Don't insult me," he said. Then, leaning close, his breath hot in her ear, he whispered, "Stick around."

3. History

The week before she started grad school—years before she became a professor of poetry—Joni Palmer had spent her student loan money on a plane ticket to Puerto Vallarta. She hoped the trip would distract her from the humiliation of getting dumped by Dr. Crabtree, a married professor who thought all her poems were about sex.

It had been the rainy season. The beach was empty. She sat under a big umbrella with an unopened notebook in her lap, staring at the choppy water and her own bare feet. That first day, between a pair of brief but furious thundershowers, a stern-looking waiter from the hotel's outdoor bar brought her a mango margarita she hadn't ordered. He wore a white smock with *Santiago* stitched in red on the pocket. He didn't speak or smile. With a dismissive wave, he insisted she take the drink.

The next morning he brought a plate of crisp French fries. For lunch, nachos and a sweating glass of horchata. In the late afternoon he showed up with a bowl of pineapple chunks and a sticky saucer of flan. She ate all of the food he gave her without really tasting it. When he finally spoke, his words sounded friendly but his face remained serious, his dark eyes intense. "Do you like to dance?" His English was perfect.

That evening, before she invited him to her room, the waiter sat beside her beneath the umbrella and together they watched the sun sink into the ocean. Already her grief had waned. A gentle rain began to fall.

"What do you write?" he said, nodding at her notebook.

"Nothing," she replied. "Poetry."

This was many years ago. But Dr. Palmer thought about it now as she rolled veggie enchiladas in the cottage she shared with her roommate, a lab assistant who had lately become her lover. She wore one of his tattered sweaters and nothing else. He was working late again, grading assignments in the closet that served as his office in the bowels of the physics building. She liked him well enough, but nothing brought her much pleasure anymore. A long time ago some part of her went missing.

4. Communications

The next morning the lab assistant told his girlfriend, Blanca, one of his secrets as they sat together on the patio of their favorite hangout, an independent coffee shop next to campus. He wore one of the ratty sweaters he had inherited from his grandfather, a famous dead physicist. She wore her favorite denim cutoffs and cowboy boots. He chain-smoked clove cigarettes. She sipped jasmine tea and worried about what he had to say. The jukebox played Bob Dylan.

What he had to say was that shortly after he met her he had a brief, passionate affair with a man who shucked oysters for a living. They fell in love one itchy night while watching stars from a blanket spread over the bed of a borrowed pickup. The lab assistant spoke dreamily about the mysteries of the universe. The oyster shucker spoke tenderly of shellfish. It felt like the start of something important. But the oyster shucker ultimately went back to his wife. Not long afterward, he died.

Having confessed, the lab assistant's face flooded with relief. He stubbed out his cigarette and leaned back in the distressed wooden chair. He stroked what little he had of a beard and awaited Blanca's reaction. Her stomach fell. Too stunned for tears, she swore instinctively in Spanish. She could think of nothing else to say while she tried to figure out how to categorize his disclosure.

"I'm surprised," she finally managed. "We live so far from the ocean."

"Forget the oysters," he said, licking his lips. "The oysters are irrelevant."

"Then why did you mention them?"

"Jesus Christ, Blanca."

"So are you telling me you're—"

"That's not what I'm saying." He lit another cigarette.

"But you must at least be—"

"God, I'm so sick of your compulsion to *label* everything," he said. "It's just something that happened."

Blanca considered this. Then shrugged. "Okay," she said, taking a sip of her lukewarm tea.

"*Okay?*"

"It's okay." She congratulated herself for how calmly she was handling this. She wanted to encourage him to tell her everything, including about the sex she suspected him of having with his roommate, a poet. "I forgive you."

The chair creaked as he stood, his brow furrowed. A thread hung from the sleeve of his pea-green sweater. He flicked his cigarette into the nearby gutter and stuffed his fingers into the pockets of his skinny jeans. Blanca suddenly understood that he meant to break up with her, and that she would never get the whole story.

"I forgive you," she repeated, softly this time.

"I didn't ask for forgiveness," he said, his eyes cold. "It's not anything to forgive."

"They why did you bring it up?"

5. Major American Playwrights

Meanwhile, in the humanities building, Dr. Crabtree watched Daisy draw penguins in the margins of her anthology. She looked lovely in his favorite maternity dress, stretched taut over a growing baby bump, and the wishbone necklace he had given her last night. The rest of his students were discussing the symbolism of meat in *A Streetcar Named Desire*.

Was he in love with her? Certainly he loved the way she strode into his dingy classroom like a queen, head high, spine straight as a book's, cornflower eyes pinning him to the floor. He loved her dark blonde braids and goofy tortoise-shell glasses, her expansive belly and the tender way she was always touching it.

He had behaved himself long enough, he thought. For so many years, after the disastrous entanglement with Joni Palmer, that sex-obsessed student poet. What a mess that was. She nearly had a nervous breakdown when he came to his senses, running off to Mexico and missing her first week of grad school. He had covered her tuition to smooth things over, and offered to pay for an abortion when he heard she was pregnant. She had made a bitter joke about "Hills Like White Elephants" and insisted on giving the baby up for adoption. The faculty lounge whispers had been intolerable. The episode nearly derailed his tenure vote. Later, his enemies in the department had successfully lobbied for her — one of their own graduates! — to fill an open teaching position. To this day she refused to look at Dr. Crabtree whenever they found themselves on the same elevator.

All those years he had behaved himself, not for lack of opportunity. He had behaved himself, for what? In hopes of someday living down his reputation as the department's stock lecher? You couldn't live something like that down. He had learned that hard lesson long before Daisy appeared in his classroom, as if by fate, the week his wife left him for good.

He didn't have to worry about Daisy, he thought. She was emotionally sturdy and discreet. She was married to her baby's father and planned to stay that way. She ignored Dr. Crabtree's pleading text messages for days at a time before finally knocking on his office door. He intended to speak to her soon about her lack of participation in class.

He loved the way her twin braids ended an inch above each of her swollen nipples, making him think of thick exclamation points. He smiled to himself until he noticed her glaring at him, her eyes blue flames behind her glasses. She laced her fingers over her belly and raised her eyebrows pointedly. The class discussion had stalled. His students were waiting. They were watching him watch her.

6. Translation

Preston was a teenage popcorn jockey at the Cinedome. He had a lazy eye and a painful crush on Blanca, the junior high school Spanish teacher who came every Friday to watch horror movies with her pregnant half-sister Daisy. Blanca wore sexy frayed shorts and shiny white cowboy boots. Daisy wore bright maternity dresses, glasses and braids. Preston wore a white vest and a red nametag.

That particular afternoon, Blanca's eyes were red-rimmed, her nose raw. He figured she had a cold. "One medium Coke," she told him, sniffling.

He wanted to take her for a ride in the used Civic his adoptive parents had given him for his birthday. He wanted to park with her at the lake, where he would impress her with a few romantic Spanish phrases he had picked up from a buddy. Then they'd make out. He didn't care if he caught her cold. In fact, he wanted to. It would underscore his devotion.

He took care to aim his good eye anywhere but at her magnetic cleavage. The other eye wandered aimlessly in its socket. Both appeared to shift by the second between different shades of green.

"Medium Coke," Blanca said again.

Preston said something to her in Spanish that made no sense, except perhaps pornographically. He smiled at her, wondering whether she would wear those boots beneath her wedding gown.

"What?" Blanca said, wiping her nose with a tissue. "What did you just say to me?"

Preston repeated the phrase he had practiced at home in the mirror, more slowly this time. Blanca stood there, frowning. Daisy's eyebrows shot up as she rubbed her big belly. Preston's face reddened. He began to doubt the trustworthiness of his Spanish-speaking buddy. But he was committed now. He decided to try once more, careful to enunciate each syllable.

"Do you have any idea what that means?" Blanca said.

"My accent's probably off."

"Right."

He turned away and poured her a large fruit punch.

7. Drama

Two weeks later, at the university president's end-of-semester party, the lab assistant held hands with Joni Palmer at the top of a grand staircase. He was miserable in his scratchy eggplant sweater. At parties he often felt like the butt of some mysterious joke. Joni yawned, snagged a meatless hors d'oeuvre from a passing tray, and asked the waiter for a glass of pinot noir. She thought about how quickly her affection for the lab assistant had waned. He thought about a cigarette.

The president's mansion was thick with half-drunk university staffers and their significant others, gathered for the president's annual summer party. Students in attendance included members of the jazz band, performing in the foyer, and Mia, the plain young woman who had passed astronomy thanks to the lab assistant's generosity. She went mute upon spotting him there, at the top of the stairs, where he stood scanning the place as if in search of an escape. That night after class, weeks ago, in his horrible office the size of her mother's pantry, he had wanted nothing more than her help grading a two-inch stack of worksheets. Still, she knew what she would have been willing to do for the extra credit. Later she would cry alone in the bathroom. But at the moment she held hands with Horacio, love of her life, who happened to be the president's nephew by marriage. She knew he had plans to propose to her tonight, after the party, over a bottle of wine at the lakeshore. But now he was eating shrimp off a cracker and staring at Dr. Palmer's bare legs.

Blanca sat on an ottoman next to the fireplace, feeling underdressed in overall shorts and her cowboy boots, wondering what to do with her empty wineglass. She didn't want to be here. Her very pregnant half-sister Daisy, invited by Dr. Crabtree, had played on Blanca's sympathies after their usual Friday matinee. The women had yet to speak to him, as he was busy schmoozing university admins in the library. It seemed like an hour since Daisy disappeared in search of a bathroom. Where *was* she? Blanca looked around and spotted her ex-boyfriend at the top of the stairs, holding hands with his roommate, the poet. She felt like flinging her wineglass into the fireplace.

Preston kept his good eye trained on her from where he was refilling at the punchbowl. He had crashed the party straight from his shift at the Cinedome, having overheard the sisters discussing it in the lobby after the movie. He was concocting a plan to accidentally bump into Blanca and then offer her a ride home, by way of the lake, in his Civic. Then they'd make out.

Dr. Palmer noticed him there, still in his vest and nametag, and nearly dropped her pinot noir. He was the spitting image of Santiago, her long-lost Mexican lover, as she had last seen him, standing barefoot in the moonlit surf on Banderas Bay, wearing his white waiter's smock. Except the eyes. Even from here she could see that the boy had *her* strangely-colored eyes, though there was something wrong with one of his. She had to remind herself to breathe.

"I need a smoke," the lab assistant said, releasing her hand. As he turned toward the balcony he saw Blanca standing next to the ottoman, wearing the stunned expression of the freshly betrayed. The two former lovers locked eyes for an instant before Blanca flung her wineglass into the fireplace. Several nearby conversations came to a halt. The lab assistant was so disconcerted that he tripped over a potted plant and tumbled down the stairs, fracturing his ankle. He landed at the feet of Daisy, who stood flushed in a yellow maternity dress, her braids in disarray, her glasses sliding down her nose.

"My water broke," she announced, clutching her giant belly.

Most of the party guests migrated to the mansion's sloping front lawn, drinks in hand, to watch as paramedics loaded Daisy and the lab assistant into a shared ambulance. The sun was setting. Dr. Crabtree stood there, wringing his hands, somehow knowing that Daisy would never again visit his office. Horacio squatted at the edge of the lawn with two glasses of wine, waiting on his beloved. Mia was inside, crying in the bathroom. Blanca was already on her way to the hospital in Daisy's Subaru. Dr. Palmer approached Preston, took his startled face in her hands, looked into his good eye and laughed through her tears. The jazz band played on.

The ambulance smelled strongly of antiseptic. The lab assistant cried into the crook of his arm while Daisy reconsidered her recent life choices. Pain provided her a temporary clarity. She had failed all but one of her classes. She took for granted her husband, a sweet, hardworking man who shrugged off her vacillating moods. She had a long habit of behaving as though nothing mattered so much as what she did with another person alone in the dark. Between contractions she thought about her mistakes and how she was in danger of never learning from them. She worried about what kind of mother she would make.

Another contraction hit. Daisy gritted her teeth and moaned.

By the time the painful tide ebbed she had resolved to make some serious changes, to curb her more unseemly tendencies.

But the paramedic was so handsome and gentle. He wiped the sweat from her brow and removed her glasses, folded them carefully and tucked them into his shirt pocket. She observed him myopically, studying his fuzzy wedding band. His hand felt so familiar in hers. Maybe they had met before, some night long ago, in her favorite dive bar full of hazy possibilities. He gave her a blurry smile. They both ignored the sniffling lab assistant. Daisy gazed up at the paramedic, her damp eyes posing the tender question. But of course they did not yet know each other at all.

8. *Composition*

The summer Joni Palmer turned eight years old, she was sent to live with her grandmother in an airy house in the country. Her parents were busy splitting up.

She spent the mornings gathering dandelions from the sprawling lawn behind her grandmother's house. She made thick bouquets of them, tying them together with string from her grandmother's sewing kit, and arranged them in clear Mason jars around the spacious kitchen. Then she sat at the counter and stared at their yellow starburst heads while her grandmother sliced fresh apples and cheese for lunch. Joni couldn't explain why she so loved the dandelions, but they were the most beautiful things in the world to her.

After lunch, she went to her bedroom and locked the door. She spent the rest of the afternoon lying barefoot on her creaky daybed, writing the same sentence again and again in one of her little notebooks.

JEREMY CALDWELL

EQUIVALENT EXCHANGE

She told me she was pregnant before
the first commercial break. We weren't married
or anything like that. She was barely old enough
to sue someone, and I still believed in sunsets
and hoped I wouldn't have to wake up. When I did
it was a few months later because of two feet
kicking in her womb. I remember telling myself to man-up.
I'm still not sure I'll ever know what that means.
She hadn't even regretted getting a tattoo yet,
or voted Democrat to piss off her parents.
It took months before I told my friends.
Stupidity looks like that, you know—feeble and easy.
I've been thinking about this television series lately.
The opening credit scene says humanity can't obtain
without first giving something of equal value in return.
I have always wondered if creation and destruction
occupy the same side of the same coin, and if, in fact,
they are something like how I destroyed her life
while making another.

COUNTRY CHURCH

The steeple top is the tallest thing in ten miles,
and a spiked iron fence hems in the small plot,
protecting it for the next hundred hard years.
Inside, pews wrinkle their way across the nave,
holding psalms communal hands grip each Sunday,
believing one thing or another can save them.
On either wall, the stained glass is stained
with dirt and the sins we only half confess to
when alone, and never when together.
Also inside, for as long as I can remember,
an elderly couple, always in the first row,
their voices as raspy as granite, hands laced
together, slightly shaking to keep each other steady.
The congregation, too, remains constant in their sum,
through the clutch of frost, the collapse of crops,
and even through the gravestones,
which are butting up against the foundation.

It's six blocks to the exit ramp, and
she rides along the shoulder.

PRECIOUS THINGS

Her collection begins with a vibrating pleasure *ring, and Susan keeps it secret. She takes out a P.O. Box the next town over, where the risk of running into someone she knows is low. She isn't sure they'll let someone under eighteen have one, so she shows them her sister's license. They hand her paperwork, and she almost enters her own information before she remembers she's supposed to be Sadie. The clerk hands her a key, and a week later, she returns. Resting in the box is a parcel wrapped in brown paper. The name of the company from which she purchased it is printed in the upper left-hand corner, but the package is anonymous, nondescript. It might contain anything really . . .*

Two girls stroll along a grassy verge at the edge of a highway, far enough that local law enforcement won't chase them off, but close enough that the blasts of truckers' horns rattle their ears as they pass. Alex suggests this route whenever they walk to the mall because she likes the attention, no matter how much she denies it.

Susan and Alex have been friends since seventh grade, and the horns have always been there. The truckers see her friend's blonde hair and pull the cord. Once they reached high school, she and Alex started making lewd gestures, laughing, but today, they walk in silence. Susan watches the cars speed by, their hulking metal bodies. She waits for the slide, the screech. She wonders what it's like: windshields caving in, glass shattering, metal twisting, plunging into her body, but she hasn't shared these thoughts — not with her parents nor Alex nor the counselor her parents force her to see Wednesday afternoons. She imagines her senses fading, vision blacking out as the blood stops pumping to her brain. Are there pieces where it happened, remnants, broken reflectors? She finds herself gazing at the ground, and Alex must notice.

"Hey," she says. "I bet you won't go in there . . ."

They're coming up to the intersection. The mall is to their left. To their right stands a gas station, an undeveloped stretch of trees and grass where Sadie had her accident, and a little further down, *Adult World*. The store was in the news for months leading up to its opening — protests, concerned citizens signing petitions to block permits, but their efforts failed. Susan has seen the place, and she's interested, but she can't show this.

"I'll go if you do," she says.

Aside from the yellow sign — black silhouettes of a man and woman, presumably nude, holding up a globe — there isn't much to suggest what's inside: racks of dirty magazines, movies. As they approach, Susan sees a placard on the door — *Patrons Must Be 21 to Enter*. But the worst they can do is chase them out. For an instant, she wonders what her parents would say, but she knows she can blame it on grief. Susan isn't concerned about using grief as a motive. She'll do whatever she wants if it makes her feel better.

The girls slide behind a rack of DVDs before the cashier can spot them. Aside from two middle-aged men, the store is empty, and Alex begins pulling movies from the shelves.

"*Let's Stain the Sheets*," she reads. "*Star Whores*."

Susan roams about, searching. At the end of an aisle, a neon glow catches her eye. There's a wall behind the counter, stocked with toys. They have vibrators of various sizes, blowup dolls folded into boxes with pictures of women in nurses' uniforms on them. They have beads and lubes, and the objects attract her — the gaudy colors, strange distortions of human anatomical design. She leans over and reaches out to touch them, but as she does, someone yells, "Hey! What do you think you're doing in here!" and Alex grabs her and they run from the store, laughing.

For the moment, Susan feels all right.

For the moment, she's not thinking of her dead sister.

Over the next two months, Susan's collection grows. Since she can't buy from the store, she orders off the Internet. Her parents had given Sadie a credit card for graduation—"in case of emergencies"—but they've forgotten about it. In those first days after the accident, when belongings were returned to the families, Susan swiped it from her sister's wallet, and since she's home all day while her parents work, she takes the bills from the mailbox and pays them without her parents' knowing. She hides her collection in a chest beneath her bed. She locks it with a built-in lock whose flimsiness begs breaking, but her parents never enter her room. The display is lovingly arranged. She owns an array of rings, each with special features—clit flickers, dual clit flickers, constricting super-soft c rings. She has an uninflated blowup doll, a wrap-around Rosie, anal beads, beads connected to c rings, c rings connected to cock rings. She even has a prostate stimulator designed to bring about what one reviewer called, "the gratest orgazm in f@#king history," a double entendre she assumes was unintended. She avoids vibrators and dildos for fear if she gets caught her mother will think she uses them to masturbate. Somehow, it seems less shameful to let her parents think she's having sex, though she doesn't have a boyfriend.

Mostly, she sees her collection as a rebellion. No black clothes and mohawk for her, not like Alex, who'd met some delinquent at a party in May and taken to wearing a leather jacket and pink streak in her hair. Her own rebellion is secretive, subversive, the speakeasy password, the French Resistance, though maybe not the French Resistance. They were heroic. Susan's just an outsider. But at least, her rebellion isn't trite.

Susan's sister was cliché, her death so typical Susan almost hates her for it—alcohol, graduation party, car crash. "It's okay to be screwed up," her mother tells her. But it doesn't seem okay. Her parents, for all their concern, are coping too well. They've joined support groups, seen therapists. They have sessions as a family, and in these sessions, it feels like her parents and counselor are teaming up on her. They urge her to share, but the more they insist, the less she's inclined.

"I miss my little girl," her mother says.

"I feel empty," her father says. "Lost . . ."

They cry, but their tears are restrained. They're both on meds to level them out. They've suggested she do the same, but she doesn't want to handle her grief. She wants to rip at her clothes and howl at the sky. She wants to burn Sadie's possessions. She wants her mother weeping at the kitchen table in a bathrobe, her father to come home from work wrecked. These are clichés she could live with. Most of all, she wants to fall apart, but she isn't interested in drugs and won't drink after what happened to Sadie. What's worse, she hasn't cried since the accident, not even at the funeral. She's worried her emotions are fading, that she's becoming cold. She'd like to talk to someone about it, just not her counselor. His insights are dim-witted, his apparent breakthroughs so textbook even a teen with a limited knowledge of Freud can predict what he's going to say.

That afternoon, she bikes to his office. She's started making up dreams with obvious symbolism for him to interpret.

"So I'm riding my bike in the street. All of a sudden, I'm on a hill. My brakes don't work, so I can't slow down. There's traffic. I'm weaving in and out, dodging cars. I'm not sure how it ends . . ."

He sits at a desk, with her on a swivel chair across from him. She plays with the strap on her bag, inside of which she's stowed a new toy.

"Could it be," he says, "that control is the issue? Could it be that you feel you have no control over what happens in your life?"

Susan bites her bottom lip and nods. Part of her wishes she could tell him the truth. She wants to ask why her parents are acting like Sadie's just moved to another town. She wants to tell him she's scared that Alex is drifting away, how they used to spend every day together, but don't anymore. She wants to tell him how, whenever she sees her friend, all Alex talks about is sex to make her jealous, but it doesn't work and Susan wishes she'd shut up. She wants to say this but worries he'll think she's crazy, and she can't deal with that—being crazy. Still, it's how she feels, with her parents coping. She wants to fess up, but she's too far into the act and he might be insulted if she does.

"Wow," she says. "I've never thought of it like that."

By summer's end, Susan wonders if she wants to get caught. Between her counselor's psychobabble and Alex's tales of debauchery, she could have hidden motives. Maybe the toys aren't a rebellion. Maybe they're a cry for help. Perhaps she keeps them hidden in her room with hopes of provoking her parents. Yet, whenever she leaves, she surrounds the box with stacks of books, thick tomes arranged to conceal it from view. If she wanted to be discovered, she'd forget to lock it, leave it out. Alex, on the other hand, tells Susan everything.

"We haven't had sex yet," she says, though Susan wonders what's stopping them.

Susan and Alex sit in her bedroom, the music turned up. Alex worries that her mother eavesdrops. She wants to tell Susan all the things she and her boyfriend have done since last week. It seems like Alex is tempting fate. Last week, she told Susan she'd given the delinquent a blowjob in the broom closet at Macy's. It sounds like Alex is just doing this so that she can tell others. What's worse is Alex punctuates each statement with a silence in which Susan suspects it's her job to ask questions. Instead, she scans Alex's yearbook, looking for pictures of Sadie.

"You need a guy," Alex says.

"I don't."

Susan flips the yearbook closed, slips it back on the shelf.

"There's this guy. He's Jim's friend. We can hang out. In a group. See if you like him . . ."

Susan reaches into her pocket to touch the ring she now carries everywhere. It's her favorite: red lacquered, wireless vibrations, a single flicker on top. She likes the smooth surface, the cool polished metal.

"Tracey McGuiness is having a party Saturday. I can bring him along . . ."

Susan knows what Alex is doing. Once the schoolyear begins, they'll see even less of each other, with Susan in the AP track and Alex not. If their boyfriends are friends, it'll give them an excuse to hang out. It's tempting, the idea of having a boyfriend. Susan likes the normalcy in it, thinks how nice it would be to feel like a regular girl.

"I can't," she says. "Maybe another time, but right now, I can't."

Some days, Susan wishes she were made of this stuff, plastics and polymers, an artificial substance engineered to bend but not break. She hasn't stepped into these halls — the narrow corridors lined with orange lockers and green and white tiles — since her sister died, and the smell of chalk dust and stale textbooks serve to augment her absence. Alex has first period free, so Susan shows up alone, slipping into the crowd, heading through the front doors. She says hello to a few acquaintances, but other than that, the only word she speaks is, "Here," seven succinct times to acknowledge her presence during attendance.

Her last class of the day is Driver's Ed. It isn't a class she'd planned to take when she made her schedule last spring, but her issues with control have come up in the sessions with her parents, and her counselor suggested she get her license. Now she's here, her bag banging against the back of her seat, the driver's manual open on her desk. She sees her presence as penance for lying to her counselor, her games gone awry.

"I think it's best she learn to drive," he'd said. "It will help her overcome her fears."

She'd been avoiding cars all summer, going by foot or bicycle whenever she could.

"Most of you see the car as freedom," the instructor tells them. "This class is one way of getting there. But freedom comes with responsibility. You'll be wielding two tons of metal, moving at high velocities. Even twenty miles an hour is enough to kill a pedestrian."

The teacher's words are slow, deliberate, his voice gruff. This wing of the school doesn't have air conditioning, so Susan's hot, lethargic, her shirt heavy with perspiration. She watches the other students. Their eyelids droop. The sun drifts through slats in the blinds, illuminating the dust motes.

"Now we'll watch some clips," the teacher says, dimming the lights.

Susan's pulse quickens. She's expecting scare tactics, images of roadside wrecks. But the first clip comes on, explaining the rudiments of safety, diagrams, actors illustrating proper technique, ten and two. When the movie shows crashes, they're simulations, using dummies. Perhaps her teacher knows about Sadie and chose the clips with care. Still, she feels dizzy. A sudden chill cuts the heat. On screen, a car rams a brick wall, the hood crumples, the windshield is blown out. The dummies thrash, go through. And Susan pictures herself as one of them, hollowed-out, empty. She has trouble catching her breath. She looks at her skin, transforming in the lucent afternoon light. There aren't any organs in there, no blood or lymph, sentience or sensation. She leans back and reaches into her pocket and rubs the ring's outline with a finger, tracing the metal prongs. It feels good, yet her pockets are tight, and as she draws her hand out, she flicks it on, vibrations filling the silence between one scene and the next.

Susan needs to feel normal again, to reassert some sense of normalcy. In August, she stops collecting. She pays off the card and closes the account, but she keeps the box under her bed and takes it out whenever she needs it. She's surprised she hasn't been exposed already. She keeps expecting her parents to call her into the dining room to talk, but when they do, it's not about the toys.

"We're having another child," her father informs her.

"You're forty-six," Susan says, looking at her mom.

"It's considered high-risk, but it's not unheard of."

Susan doesn't care. If they need it, why not? Susan needs other things. She wonders what advice Sadie would give her. Susan and Sadie hadn't moved in the same circles. But Sadie had never ignored her. Susan could have used her help right now, with Alex being how she was, an incompetent shrink, her parents replacing the child they lost. She's embarrassed she turned her ring on in class, though no one noticed, and if they had, they hadn't known what it was.

"So what?" she hears Sadie say, her voice clear in a way her face no longer is. "You turned on your cock ring in Driver's Ed. There's life after this."

Her sister's mind was always on the future. Sadie was popular, but she wanted more from life. College, then career. Career, then family. Sadie had picked her college in ninth grade—NYU.

"I want to do the big city, live it up."

And she'd worked to get the grades and got in. Only she never went.

"You have to get out more," Sadie would say, tossing her hair, her relaxed manner making her trite diagnosis seem profound. And maybe it's true. Maybe Susan's kept to herself too long, nursing her pain. Maybe she needs to get out. She calls Alex.

"Hey," she says, "you know that party? Could we go? Just me and you?"

The night of the party, Susan's thinking of Sadie, of how she died. It's not the same party, not the same night, but she's nervous. She almost regrets her decision to call Alex but for one thing: she gets to spend the evening with her friend, no delinquent. Susan and Alex have arranged to meet there. Neither has their license, which offers Susan some relief, since neither has to drive home, and Susan searches her closet for something to wear.

When Susan arrives, she feels better. Alex is already there, and she and Susan carve out a seat on the sofa where they catch up on the week, discuss classes, teachers.

"I have Thompson for Chemistry," Susan says. "I like him. He's funny."

"I think he's hot," Alex says.

"He's got to be sixty years old!"

"Well, he's hot in that charming old man kind of way. I'd like to rub his bald head."

They're laughing, and all the while, Susan tries not to think of Sadie, of how the night she died she'd probably done these things—lingered in choosing her clothes, met up with friends, talked, laughed. She'd probably had a good time. People stand around, listening to music, chatting, with red plastic cups in their hands. But Alex refrains and Susan loves her for this. They used to drink, she and Alex, at the parties they'd gone to before. But now they don't.

After a while, they get up, move about, mingle. They stop before a set of sliding glass doors that lead out back to a pool. Susan's watching the glistening blue waters, the way the waves lap at the concrete lip, when someone slaps the glass. She jumps back and finds herself face-to-face with the delinquent and one of his friends. The boys open the door, and Susan reaches for her pocket.

"Did you know they were coming?" she asks.

"No, I swear," Alex says. "Jim mentioned they might stop by, but I didn't invite him."

Jim grabs Alex by the waist as Susan leaves. It doesn't matter if Alex planned this or not. She's back to being dull Susan, sad Susan, Susan who can't cope.

She pulls her cardigan close about her shoulders and spots a bike in the yard. She doesn't know whose it is, but she only plans to borrow it. She's never been to the spot where Sadie died, the exact spot, but as her feet touch the pedals, she knows that's where she's headed.

It's six blocks to the exit ramp, and she rides along the shoulder. As she enters the freeway, cars honk and pass. She keeps a steady pace, gravel crunching beneath her tires. It's dark, near midnight, but the moon is lighting her way.

The crash happened four months ago, a few hundred yards down the road from *Adult World*. The region is grassy, peppered by oak and pine, and that's what did it. Sadie's boyfriend had lost control of the wheel, they were moving at high speed, they'd veered off the road. Had it been a plain field, they might have been okay, but they'd hit a tree.

Susan drops the bike. There's a divot the size of a tire, it might be a track. She picks up a stick and starts whipping the overgrown grass, looking for traces of taillights, pieces of the wreck, but the world has moved on, even if she can't. Had Sadie been scared? Did she know what was happening? The car had caught fire. The service was closed-casket. Had it scorched the tree?

She stops beside a sycamore and places her hand on the trunk, looking for blackened bark. At its base is a red piece of plastic. She bends and picks it up, tracing its rigid edge. *This is it*, she thinks, *all that's left*. She wants to cry but can't. She's suddenly weak. She lies down and looks up at the sky. She takes out her ring and sets it atop her chest to hum. Her heart is dead, dried and withered, but in the dark of night, as she touches her breast, she pretends that it still knows how to beat.

SAM ASHER is a 30-year-old writer living in New York City, where he tolerates the winters awaiting the barely more tolerable summers.

MARIE-ANDRÉE AUCLAIR'S poems have appeared in a variety of print and online literary publications such as *Apeiron*, *Harpur Palate*, *Understorey*, *Existere*, *Hart House Review*, *The Coachella Review*, and others. Her chapbook *Contrails* was released by In/Words Magazine and Press/Ottawa. She lives in Canada and is working on another chapbook.

GAYLORD BREWER is a professor at Middle Tennessee State University, where he founded and for more than 20 years edited the journal *Poems & Plays*. His most recent books are the cookbook-memoir *The Poet's Guide to Food, Drink, & Desire* (Stephen F. Austin, 2015) and a tenth collection of poetry, *The Feral Condition* (Negative Capability, 2018).

JEREMY CALDWELL'S writing has been published in *Poetry Quarterly*, *Comstock Review*, *Work Literary Magazine*, and *Prairie Schooner*, among others. He has an M.A. in Creative Writing from the University of Nebraska-Lincoln, and currently works as an Academic Specialist for Doane University in Crete, Nebraska.

LYNNETTE CURTIS is a freelance writer who lives in Las Vegas, Nevada, and studies fiction in the M.F.A. Program for Writers at Warren Wilson College. Her creative work has appeared in *New South* and *The Other Stories*. She won the 2018 Irene Adler Scholarship for women writers.

KERRY JAMES EVANS is the recipient of a 2015 NEA Fellowship, a Walter E. Dakin Fellowship from Sewanee Writers' Conference, and his poems have appeared in *Agni*, *New*

England Review, *Ploughshares*, and many other journals. He is the author of *Bangalore* (Copper Canyon) and an Assistant Professor of English at Tuskegee University.

ADAM GNUSE received an M.F.A. in fiction from UNC Wilmington and was a 2018 *Kenyon Review* Summer Workshop Peter Taylor fellow. His writing has appeared or is forthcoming in *Guernica*, *The Los Angeles Review Online*, *New South*, *Passages North*, *The Wisconsin Review*, and other magazines. You can reach him at adamgnuse.com.

MEREDITH DAVIES HADAWAY is the author of three poetry collections. Her most recent, *At the Narrows*, won the 2015 Delmarva Book Prize. She is a former Rose O'Neill Writer-in-Residence at Washington College, where she taught English and creative writing in addition to serving as vice president for communications and marketing.

ANDREW HAMM is a writer and journalist who lives in Bethesda, Maryland. By day he manages SCOTUSblog, a website that covers the U.S. Supreme Court, and by night he serves as the online editor for *Little Patuxent Review*, a literary journal published in Columbia, Maryland. He is a graduate of the Johns Hopkins Masters of Writing Program, and his online publications include *Traces* and *On Tap Magazine*.

PAUL HANEY'S work has appeared in *The Cincinnati Review*, *Fourth Genre*, *Slate*, *Boston Globe Magazine*, *Essay Daily*, and elsewhere. Originally from Orlando, he lives and teaches writing in Boston, where he served as Editor-in-Chief of *Redivider* while earning his MFA from Emerson College. Now he's working on a book-length memoir-slash-critical study of Bob Dylan. Follow him @paulhaney.

CLAIRE HERO is the author of the full-length poetry collection *Sing, Mongrel* and three chapbooks: *afterpastures*, winner of the 2008 *Caketrain* Chapbook competition, *Cabinet*, and *Dollyland*. Her poems and stories have appeared or are forthcoming in such journals as *Bennington Review*, *Black Candies*, *Black Warrior Review*, *The Cincinnati Review*, *Copper Nickel*, *Denver Quarterly*, and *Fairy Tale Review*.

J.M. JONES works as a writer and editor in Philadelphia. His short fiction and nonfiction have appeared in *The Normal School*, *Phoebe*, *The Southeast Review*, and *Barrelhouse*. For more, please see jasonmjones.net.

HOLLY KARAPETKOVA'S poetry, prose, and translations from Bulgarian have appeared recently in *Prairie Schooner*, *The Nashville Review*, *The Southern Review*, and other places. Her second book, *Towline*, won the Vern Rutsala Poetry Prize and was published by Cloudbank Books.

CINDY KING'S recent publications include poems in *The Sun*, *Callaloo*, *North American Review*, *The Cincinnati Review*, *River Styx*, and elsewhere. Her book-length poetry manuscript, *Zoonotic*, will be published by Tinderbox Editions in 2020. Her chapbook, *Easy Street*, will be published by Dancing Girl Press in March 2019. She was born in Cleveland, Ohio and grew up swimming in the shadows of the hyperboloid cooling towers on the shores of Lake Erie. At 23 she moved to Mississippi and has lived most of her life south of the Mason-Dixon as a naturalized Southerner. Perpetually bewildered, she currently lives in Southern Utah, where she doesn't know a butte from a bluff. A frequent backdrop for sci-fi features, the region's landscape isn't the only thing that makes her feel as if she's living on another planet. She is an Assistant Professor of Creative Writing at Dixie State University and Editor of *The Southern Quill*.

CHARLENE LANGFUR is an organic gardener, a rescued dog advocate, a Syracuse University Graduate Writing Fellowship holder, and her most recent publications include an essay in *Still Point Arts Quarterly* called "Chasing Home," a poem in *Turtle Island Responds / Room Magazine*, and a series of poems in *Hawk & Handsaw – Journal of Creative Sustainability* in December 2018.

APRIL LINDNER is the author of two poetry collections, *Skin* (Texas Tech University Press) and *This Bed Our Bodies Shaped* (Able Muse Press). She also has published three young adult novels: *Jane*, *Catherine*, and *Love, Lucy*, all with Poppy/Little, Brown Young Reader. Her digital-exclusive novella, *Far from Over*, was published by NOVL. She teaches writing at Saint Joseph's University and lives in Lambertville, New Jersey.

GEORGE LOONEY'S recent books include *Hermits in Our Own Flesh: The Epistles of an Anonymous Monk*, *Meditations Before the Windows Fail*, the book-length poem *Structures the Wind Sings Through*, *Monks Beginning to Waltz*, and *A Short Bestiary of Love and Madness*. His novel *Report from a Place of Burning* was co-winner of The Leapfrog Press Fiction Award and will be published in 2018. He is the founder of the B.F.A. in Creative Writing Program at Penn State Erie, editor-in-chief of the international literary journal *Lake Effect*, translation editor of *Mid-American Review*, and co-founder of the original Chautauqua Writers' Festival.

CHLOE MARTINEZ'S poetry has appeared in *The Collagist*, *Crab Orchard Review*, *The American Journal of Poetry*, and elsewhere, and has been nominated for a Pushcart Prize. A graduate of Boston University's Creative Writing M.A. and the M.F.A. for Writers at Warren Wilson College, she lives in Claremont, CA, where she teaches on South Asian religions at Claremont McKenna College. See more of her work at www.chloeAVmartinez.com.

DEREK MONG is the author of two collections from Saturnalia Books — *Other Romes* and *The Identity Thief* — as well as a chapbook, *The Ego and the Empiricist*, a finalist for the Two Sylvias Press Chapbook Prize. The Byron K. Trippet Assistant Professor of English at Wabash College, he blogs at *Kenyon Review Online* and writes the occasional essay-review for *The Gettysburg Review*. New poetry and essays can be found in *Free Verse, Verse Daily, Kenyon Review Online*, and *The Hopwood Poets Revisited: Sixteen Major Award Winners*. A long poem is forthcoming in *At Length*. He and his wife, Anne O. Fisher, received the 2018 Cliff Becker Translation Award for *The Joyous Science: Selected Poems of Maxim Amelin*, now out from White Pine Press. They live in Indiana with their son.

DAVID MORSE'S poems have appeared in *Blue Collar Review, Comstock Review, Friends Journal, The Kerf, Potomac Review, Tiger's Eye*, and other journals. His essays have appeared in *Boulevard, Esquire, Green Mountains Review, Salon*, and elsewhere. His novel, *The Iron Bridge*, was published by Harcourt Brace. A human rights activist, novelist, and award-winning journalist, he divides his time between writing poetry and restoring an eighteenth-century farmhouse in eastern Connecticut, where crows speak to him regularly.

KEVIN PHAN is a Vietnamese-American graduate of the University of Michigan with an M.F.A. in Creative Writing in 2013 & from the University of Iowa with a B.A. in English Literature in 2005. He is a former Helen Zell Writers' Program Postgraduate Fellow at the University of Michigan, where he won the Theodore Roethke & Bain-Swiggett Poetry Prizes. His work has been featured (or is forthcoming) in *Columbia Review,*

Poetry Northwest, Georgia Review, Conjunctions (online), *Crab Orchard Review, Fence, Pleiades, Gulf Coast, Colorado Review, SubTropics, Crazyhorse, Hayden's Ferry Review,* & elsewhere. His first collection of poetry was recently selected as a semi-finalist for the *Crab Orchard* Open Poetry Competition, a finalist for the *Crab Orchard* First Book Prize, & as a finalist for the *Colorado Review* Poetry Prize. Currently, he earns wages through the City of Boulder, in the foothills of Colorado, where he mitigates noxious weeds, maintains softball fields, & cuts the turf. He's tall. Also, a multilingual Capricorn.

A.R. Robins received her M.A. at Southeast Missouri State University. Her fiction is published or forthcoming in *Moon City Review, Opossum, The Big Muddy, The Swamp,* and others. Her poetry is published or forthcoming in *Crack the Spine, Trailer Park Quarterly, The Cape Rock, Atlas and Alice,* and others.

Erin Saxon is an M.F.A. candidate at the University of Missouri-Kansas City. Her work has recently appeared in *Ekphrasis, The Mulberry Fork Review,* and the *Kansas City Star.* She teaches creative writing at Literacy KC, a non-profit that helps adults improve their literacy skills.

Andrew Stallings lives with his wife and their children at Deerfield Academy, a boarding prep high school in Western Massachusetts, where he teaches poetry and coaches cross country and track. His first two collections of poetry, *To the Heart of the World* (2014) and *Paradise* (2018) have both been published by Rescue Press. He formerly edited *THERMOS,* a journal of poetry, and poems from *Paradise* have been published online and in print in over fifty different literary journals during the last two years.

LAURA SWEENEY facilitates Writers for Life in central Iowa. She represented the Iowa Arts Council at the First International Teaching Artist's Conference in Oslo, Norway. Her recent and forthcoming poems appear in *Hawaii Pacific Review, Split Rock Review, Mobius, Tipton Poetry Journal, Hedge Apple, Pilgrimage, Appalachia, Edify Fiction,* and the anthologies *Nuclear Impact; Beer, Wine, & Spirits;* and *Vanguard: Exercises for the Creative Writing Classroom.* She is associate editor for *Eastern Iowa Review.*

DEVON TOMASULO has a Doctor of Letters degree in writing and literature from Drew University as well as an M.F.A. from Pacific University and a B.A. in writing from the University of Massachusetts, Amherst. She has also recently graduated from the Master in Applied Positive Psychology at the University of Pennsylvania, studying the connection between the humanities and well-being. Tomasulo's poetry has appeared in *Bitter Oleander* and *Euphony Journal,* and is forthcoming in *The Round.* She has also published articles and essays about poetry on PsychCentral.com. Tomasulo was a part of a panel presenting on Language and Rhetoric in Large-Scale Writing Assessment at the 2018 Annual Convention of the Conference on College Composition and Communication, and will be presenting on the future of Performance Writing Assessment at the 2019 conference.

READ TRAMMEL received an M.F.A. in Creative Writing from the University of Montana. His work has been published in *Bright Bones: An Anthology of Contemporary Montana Writing, Adelaide Literary Magazine, Driftwood Press, Yale Angler's Journal, Solstice Literary Magazine,* and *Foothills Literary Journal.*

KAREN J. WEYANT'S poems and essays have appeared in *The Briar Cliff Review, Chautauqua, cream city review, Copper Nickel, Lake Effect, Poetry East, Punctuate, Rattle, River Styx, Stoneboat,* and *Whiskey Island.* The author of two poetry chapbooks, she is an Associate Professor of English at Jamestown Community College in Jamestown, New York.

CPSIA information can be obtained
at www.ICGtesting.com
Printed in the USA
FSHW010703120319